The Mystery of the Cursed Castle

A Gentleman Detective Mystery

Evelyn James

Red Raven Publications 2024
www.sophie-jackson.com

Contents

One

Bainbridge finished the last line on the letter he was writing.

"...and this concludes my findings on the sabotage of your carriage and the reason for your horses suddenly slipping their harnesses and departing, leaving you stranded in the middle of the High Street."

Bainbridge paused as he considered how to phrase what he wished to say next. It was never easy to tell a wealthy client that it was due to a certain penny-pinching neglect on their part that an unfortunate inconvenience had occurred.

"The malfunction was not due to any deliberate malicious action by an unknown individual. Rather, it was the natural deterioration of a set of harness straps that had been in use for too many years. The evidence I have gathered from your coachman and those who collected your horses after the incident has proven to me conclusively that it was just a matter of time before the harnesses snapped."

Again, Bainbridge paused.

He was now in the awkward position of explaining to his client that they had been rather stingy when it came to replacing the carriage harness for their horses and this had resulted in the malfunction of the leather straps. The coachman had told him that the harness had been in use for far too long, longer than he could remember, which was a worrying sign. It was virtually antique, and the coachman had repeatedly informed his employer that it was on the cusp of disintegrating. His employer, however, refused to believe him and when the malfunction eventually occurred, he somewhat inevitably still refused to accept that it was his own miserliness that was the cause.

He had stumbled out of his carriage, shaking his fist, and declaring that someone had sabotaged his horses. He followed that up by seeking out Colonel Bainbridge and insisting he investigate the matter.

The irony was that though Bainbridge's services wouldn't cost quite as much as a new set of harnesses for the horses, it was a wholly unnecessary expense. His fee would have gone a long way to buying new tack. Instead of accepting the obvious, the man decided that he wanted to prove to himself that it wasn't his fault.

The harness had malfunctioned due to the actions of someone else; some nefarious and unnamed opponent.

Bainbridge was taking great care to outline to his client as delicately as he could manage that the man would have been better spending his money on new leather tack than a private detective.

And then he was going to mention his fee and how he expected his bill to be paid in a timely fashion.

"I am satisfied that there was no ulterior motive for the harness snapping and that no one is attempting to endanger your life as you feared initially when we met. I have obtained various proofs that I will enclose in this letter to confirm to you the matter. I consider the case now resolved and I also include with it my bill."

Bainbridge hesitated; that last line sounded rather forthright. He was deeply concerned that his client might decide that if Bainbridge could not prove his carriage was sabotaged, he had not earned his fee.

"My bill demonstrates the hours I have spent investigating this

matter and speaking to various people, and I do expect it to be paid promptly, even though the conclusion is perhaps not what you desired."

That didn't sound right either.

He paused again. Maybe he shouldn't mention the bill at all? Just enclose it with the letter and work on the assumption it would be paid. Then if his client argued over paying him, he would send his niece Victoria after the gentleman. Victoria was very good at making reluctant clients pay up. She stormed around to the person's house, demanding to know why their bill was overdue. For some reason, no one ever denied her, and money was usually quickly forthcoming, often with a little extra just to get her off the doorstep.

Bainbridge admitted that he was somewhat cowardly when it came to asking for money. He put down his own qualms over asking for money, to the fact he had been raised a gentleman, and gentlemen do not ask for money. They are just supposed to always have it.

Victoria, who was even more of a gentlewoman than he was a gentleman, had also been raised in the lap of luxury, but she did not share his qualms. She wanted to remain in the lap of luxury, and this was not currently occurring while Bainbridge dithered over sending bills to his clientele. She therefore had picked up the slack.

In the past, it had been Houston Fairchild, Bainbridge's deceased business partner who had been responsible for collecting money from reluctant clients. Houston was American and when he swaggered up to a door and demanded in his best American drawl that he fancied there had been an oversight in paying his bill, he was never questioned. The gun he usually had sitting on his hip probably went a long way to achieving this result, even if it was never loaded.

Bainbridge decided the letter was not right after all. He put it to one side and began again. He wouldn't mention anything about the possibility of his bill not being paid. He would assumed it would be paid on time and leave the rest to Victoria.

Downstairs, he heard the front doorbell ring.

He was upstairs in his study; a rather dark room tucked at the back of the house with a lot of heavy bookshelves and a dark mahogany desk. It could seem a little gloomy, but he found it a good place to be introspective. He often had his best revelations about his cases in this room. It was also one of the quieter areas of the house. He usually wasn't interrupted by his housekeeper, Mrs Huggins, when he was in his study, which made it the ideal retreat when he wanted to get away from everyone.

However, the ringing of the doorbell had distracted him, and he now had one ear pricked as he listened for Mrs Huggins wandering along the hall to answer it. He quickly ran through his mind who might be delivering goods at this hour and on this particular day of the week, and concluded they were not expecting anything. It therefore seemed very likely that the visitor was going to be someone with a new case for him.

Unless it was one of those new Christian societies who tended to come around unannounced with religious pamphlets. He read one only the other day which had declared to him that gluttony was the worst sin of their society. The lady who gave it to him was very primly dressed and had glared at him as he stood in the doorway in his dressing gown that was not quite big enough these days to hide his sizeable belly. He considered the pamphlet was a personal insult.

Bainbridge had politely informed her that he was quite satisfied that he did not suffer from the sin of gluttony, but if he ever felt it coming over him, he would be sure to let her know. Then handed her back the pamphlet and slammed the door in her face.

That had been one of the unfortunate days when Mrs Huggins had an afternoon off, forcing him to answer his own door. After the unsettling incident, he had decided that if Mrs Huggins wasn't present he would leave Victoria to door opening duties, and if his niece wasn't present either, well, he would have to hope the person came back another time.

Bainbridge picked up a fresh sheet of paper, made sure his pen was full of ink and was about to start again on the letter, but his hand hovered over the blank sheet as he listened to what was going on downstairs.

He could hear the muffled tones of a conversation. It must be someone wanting him, he thought to himself. The length of time the conversation was going on without Mrs Huggins slamming the door or swearing at the visitor gave him hope.

It should be pointed out that Mrs Huggins claimed she had never sworn a curse word in her life, but the tone in which she used what would otherwise be quite innocent words could assure even the densest of callers quite what she meant by them.

Bainbridge decided that the person downstairs must be a potential client, and his curiosity got the better of him. Putting down his pen, he headed to the door of his study and opened it a fraction. As he did so, his eyes lifted and he glanced across the landing, noticing that Victoria's bedroom door was also a fraction ajar. She had had the same idea, and she too was pretending not to be listening to what was going on downstairs.

Their eyes met and, in unspoken agreement, they both stepped onto the landing, looking slightly abashed and sheepish. They had both been caught out eavesdropping. They stood in silence either side of the stair banisters, listening to what was going on downstairs.

"As you can see, it is a very urgent matter that I speak with the Colonel."

"And as I say, I shall see if the Colonel is free, but I make no promises. You can wait for him in the front drawing room."

That was Mrs Huggins being her usual prim and proper self. They all knew that Bainbridge was always available for a new case. He just couldn't resist. As long as he was in the house, he would speak to anyone bringing him a mystery.

There was the sound of feet moving and someone shuffled across to the front drawing room. This was the signal to Bainbridge and Victoria to hasten back into their respective rooms as Mrs Huggins was now heading up the stairs to seek them out.

Mrs Huggins knocked politely on the colonel's study door, and he pretended to be absorbed writing his letter when he called out for her to enter.

"There is a gentleman downstairs, Colonel, says he has a case for you, but I'm not sure it's the sort of thing you want to deal with. I nearly turned him away."

Mrs Huggins turning away a case was virtually unheard of. She knew that Bainbridge was interested in even the most bizarre of mysteries.

Bainbridge now spun around in his chair and glanced at her.

"Why would you say that, Mrs Huggins?"

"Well, because the gentleman was spouting an awful lot of nonsense," Mrs Huggins said. "I don't hold with all this nonsense about spirits and evil spectres haunting ruins."

"Now you have my attention, Mrs Huggins. What precisely was the gentleman telling you?"

"He said it was a matter of life and death, which seemed extraordinary to me. He has recently inherited a house and with it comes a ruined castle. He says the castle is haunted by a malignant entity and he wants someone to get rid of it."

"That sounds more like the work of a priest than it does a private detective," Bainbridge mumbled.

"I thought the fellow looked decidedly shifty. Rather pale, if you see my meaning. The sort of fellow who spends too much time indoors reading books."

"Even so, Mrs Huggins, the fellow has come to seek me out and it seems only proper that I should speak to him and determine whether I can assist him in this matter."

Bainbridge was already thinking that a case involving malignant entities, (which of course were not real) was certainly more exciting than the case of an old horse harness snapping simply because the master of the house was mean fisted with money.

"He did also mention that someone had died," Mrs Huggins grumbled again. "Which is really why I allowed him to stay."

"There has been a murder as well," Bainbridge was intrigued indeed. "I must see him at once."

Mrs Huggins moved aside, and Bainbridge started to head down the stairs as Victoria emerged from her bedroom.

"You were of course going to ask me to accompany you, weren't you?" She called from over the banister.

Bainbridge paused halfway down the stairs. He had completely forgotten about his niece.

Victoria Bovington had joined him a couple of years ago after breaking off her engagement to a certain gentleman who had been unfaithful to her. At the time she had asked to become his assistant, her mother had been appalled but that only made Victoria even more determined to become a private detective. It also happened that at the time she had come to Bainbridge, he was in somewhat of the doldrums. He had recently lost his partner, Houston Fairchild who had been tragically shot. The culprits for Houston's murder were still at large and Bainbridge had found consolation in having his niece at his side to help him through his grief.

He was reluctantly prepared to admit that she was shaping up into quite a good private detective.

Victoria was not what anyone would expect of someone who investigated what could sometimes be quite grisly crimes. She looked every inch the fashionable gentlewomen, with her slender waist, pretty face and dazzling youthfulness. But she was getting better and better at apprehending criminals.

Bainbridge, who was on the wrong side of sixty and ate one too many meals a day, valued having someone who was slightly more athletic at his side – Bainbridge could not recall the last time it had been necessary for him to run. He was not even sure if his legs would remember how to do it.

However, he did occasionally forget all about his niece in his enthusiasm for a new case; not that he would ever admit that.

"Naturally I was going to summon you," he lied. "I was just going to determine if this was a matter worthy of us investigating before I bothered you. Mrs Huggins tells me she is not convinced there is a case here at all, and I do value Miss Huggins' opinion on these matters."

Victoria cast a look towards the housekeeper. In response Mrs Huggins, who was an older middle-aged woman with dense grey hair pulled back into a bun, folded her arms across her robust chest, and glowered defiantly at Victoria, daring her to suggest that a mere housekeeper wouldn't be capable of determining if a case were worthy or not.

"Mrs Huggins has been with me so many years now she is pretty good at working out whether a case deserves attention or not. This one, she feels, might not warrant a full investigation, and I didn't like to trouble you until I was sure there was anything to discuss."

"Well, as I am here already, I shall come down with you anyway. It is not a bother," Victoria said firmly.

The reality was that she had been desperate for a distraction. She was bored out of her mind. The recent case of the 'sabotaged' horse harness had not required her attention, so she had been trying to keep up with the household bookkeeping. This was an endeavour that always made her head hurt and depressed her for Bainbridge had very little concept of how money worked. He also had very little idea of how much he earned compared to how much he spent.

To Victoria's way of thinking, they were not in a position to turn away any case that came their way. They needed all the mysteries they could solve to at least try to keep them solvent.

She followed Bainbridge downstairs, and they went immediately into the drawing room where Mrs Huggins had left their guest. The gentleman was tall and lanky. He had an unfortunate overbite which was not improved by the bristly moustache he had grown in an endeavour to make his visage slightly more appealing. His gaunt cheeks, pointed chin, and heavy eyebrows all added to an appearance that could at best be remarked upon as being eccentric and distinctive. Certainly, it was not attractive.

He was dressed very finely, however. His outfit was clearly new and of the latest design. Victoria was not so familiar with men's tailors as she was ladies' haberdashers, but she could have made a good guess at where he had got the suit from, and who had made it. She noticed that the jacket had a purple silk lining, and his waistcoat had dainty stitching around the buttonholes. All the little details that told her it was a very well-tailored suit. Their guest had taken off his top hat and was now placing a monocle in front of his right eye. When he saw them, he stepped forward and bowed, the monocle immediately falling off his face. It was prevented from hitting the floor by a chain that attached to his waistcoat.

"I apologise if I am disrupting your day," he said at once to Bainbridge. "Your housekeeper informed me you are extremely busy. But I really hoped you would see me."

"Mrs Huggins has told me this is a matter of life and death," Bainbridge remarked. "I am always willing to listen to cases like that. Allow me to introduce my niece, Victoria Bovington, who assists me in all my cases."

The biggest test any client who came to Bainbridge had to face was the moment when they decided how they were going to respond to Victoria's presence. She had experienced numerous reactions over the past couple of years. She had had a few gentlemen who had just said that they had no interest in a woman looking into their case. A couple had even stormed out when Bainbridge had made it plain that Victoria would be investigating alongside him.

Others, usually of a younger generation, or those who recognised how attractive Victoria were, became immensely concerned about the possibility of any harm befalling her while she was involved with the mystery they had brought to Bainbridge. Not to mention more than one had attempted to flirt with her and even invited her out for dinner.

A couple of the latter had even been married at the time, but seemed to think that being a private detective meant that Victoria had a different set of morals compared to other women of her class.

The gentleman before them right now, did not even show a moment of uncertainty as Victoria was introduced to him. He gave another deep bow in her direction.

"I should be glad to have you both aboard on this matter. The more eyes on this incident the better. I am Lord Brooksby. Lord Augustus Brooksby, to be precise. Newly risen to that title after the unfortunate demise of my father. In actual fact, it's his death that I wish to speak to you about. You see, I think he was killed by a phantom and I think that same phantom wants to kill me next."

Two

Lord Brooksby began to pace back and forth across the drawing room carpet. His statement had not drawn an immediate gasp of shock from Victoria and Bainbridge as he had anticipated.

It was not the first time that Bainbridge had been called in to investigate the sudden death of a parent, especially among the nobility. There were always matters flaring up in response to things such as inheritance. He therefore was not immediately surprised by what he had been told.

"It would be best if you took a seat, Lord Brooksby, and explained to us how this all came about," Bainbridge suggested to him, motioning with his hand to an armchair. Bainbridge also wanted to be seated; he never remained standing for very long unless he couldn't help it. But it was impolite to sit down before a guest.

Brooksby glanced at the chair as if it might eat him, then he reluctantly settled in it. Victoria and Bainbridge took places on the sofa set at right angles to the armchair.

"I suppose it all began around a year ago," Brooksby began. "That was when my father bought the house in Bungay. He wasn't actually interested in the house itself, but he was very interested in the ruined castle that came along with the property. The house is a rather small cottage, not a place we could live. It once was inhabited by a local writer, a lady, who used it as a retreat and even wrote a novel about the ruins adjoining it.

"As I say, it was not the house that interested my father, but the castle ruins that were sold with it. The ruins of Bungay Castle are quite famous in the area. They are both picturesque as well as quite haunting in appearance."

"I am familiar with the ruins," Bainbridge nodded. "I recall many years ago going to visit them. There were a number of young ladies present in the grounds who took the opportunity to draw and paint copies of the structure."

"The castle certainly has its charms," Brooksby declared. "My father had admired it for many, many years. When the opportunity arose to buy the cottage that was attached to it, and thus to own the ruins, he simply could not resist."

"What was his intention for the property?" Victoria asked. "He clearly was not going to live there."

"No, quite," Brooksby smiled at her. "My mother would never hear of it. What he was interested in was turning the castle into something of a visitor attraction. He had this notion that he could make it into a beautiful place with gardens all around it that people could come and visit. They could take tea there and admire the ruins. My father had always been fascinated by our local history and believed that we should encourage people to pay more attention to it than we do. He used to say that everything to do with preserving historical buildings in this country was so slapdash. Ruins were just left to rot away, when they could be studied and shown to the public so that they could better understand what our ancestors were truly capable of. I agree with him in this regard. I have always been fascinated by history myself.

"Acquiring the property at Bungay gave him the opportunity to create a better understanding of our medieval heritage in the general populace. I mentioned the book written about the castle. My father thought that novel would be a good way of getting people to come and see the property. He was going to see if a periodical would serialise it if he could get the rights for it, of course. That would attract people to the castle, and he had all manner of plans how to entertain and educate them once they were there. He was going to put a roof over sections of it to protect the interior and even thought about doing things such as open-air plays inside the walls.

My father's mind was truly alive with ideas. He was always keen to be doing something new. He wanted to inspire people. He wanted the next generation to appreciate what was all around them."

"It certainly sounds a worthy endeavour," Bainbridge nodded at him. "But I take it things have not gone to plan."

"It all began very well," Brooksby explained. "As I say, we acquired the castle about a year ago. Since that time we've been gradually working on improving it. Putting it into a condition that makes it suitable for visitors. Some of the stonework was dangerously loose in places and needed to be shored up or removed. We began to create pathways for people to walk along rather than having to go across the grass. There are further steps we are planning, such as putting up a bandstand and refurbishing the cottage to enable it to be used as a tearoom. There's been quite a bit of work happening at the site since we bought it, and for the first six months or so, this seemed to cause no bother to anybody. Of course, the locals would come along and see what we were up to. But no one seemed troubled.

"Then it came to May. That was when my father had hoped to first begin welcoming paying visitors. You see, as much as he wanted the site to be educational, he also recognised that it was something of a money pit and he needed to recoup some of the great costs he had expended on its refurbishment. This was about the time that things started to go wrong. If my father was going to charge people to visit the castle and look about the ruins, then it was necessary to prevent people accessing the site without permission.

"He therefore had a sturdy fence put up around it consisting of iron railings, the sort you see around a private park, with a sturdy gate in the middle. The gate had an even sturdier padlock, and a caretaker was installed in the cottage where he could watch for any trespassers.

"The caretaker happens to be an old retainer of the family who was struggling with his regular household duties, which is why my father thought a slightly easier role would suit him. All he has to do is sit up in his rooms and watch the grounds. When the time comes for visitors to arrive, he will open the gates, collect money for the tickets and welcome them in. We never anticipated there would be any problem."

"I am going to surmise, Lord Brooksby, that this new arrangement has caused immediate trouble among the locals who were used to walking around the castle as they pleased," Victoria spoke.

Lord Brooksby nodded his head sadly.

"The locals were familiar with the castle being open at all times. There had never been any issue with the previous occupants. The lady writer who I mentioned did not live in the cottage. She only occupied it when she wished to write. The rest of the time it was locked up. The locals have always considered the castle something that belongs to them rather than to an individual. Part of the reason my father wanted to fence it off was because some of the locals used it for, well... *disreputable* activities. We would find beer bottles discarded in the ruins, and we had been told that some of the local lads liked to rendezvous with their lady friends there."

"But I don't suppose it was just those sorts of people who used the castle and considered it a good place to walk," Victoria pressed him.

"Certainly not. There are a number of local dog walkers who like to use the green and let their dog dogs run around the ruins. And some of the local farmers were used to using the grounds for extra grazing for their sheep at certain times of the year. We even had one lady who was of an artistic nature, who told us that she always went to the castle at certain times of the year to watch the sunrise and was now very displeased that she would be unable to do so. I suppose, in hindsight, we could have handled things somewhat better. But it has to be noted that the land is private property, it has never been common land. We own it and have every right to put a fence around it."

"Legal rights compared to what people consider their cultural rights often do not hold weight," Bainbridge told him gently. "Have you had any trouble from the locals?"

"A little, but nothing terribly serious. Mostly it has been verbal protests and letters, there was a short campaign in the local newspaper, but nothing came of it. The caretaker who we have stationed in the cottage has been wholly untroubled. He has actually been quite good at getting local people on his side. He goes to the pub quite often and drinks with some of the lads. I believe he's won them over somewhat."

"Then who precisely has caused you trouble?" Bainbridge persisted. "And how has this resulted in what you believe was the untimely death of your father?"

Lord Brooksby took a deep breath.

"From the moment we acquired the castle... No, let me take that back, long before we acquired the castle, we knew of its reputation of being severely haunted. The legend has it that one of the former occupants of the castle fell afoul of the monarchy and literally lost his head. He is said to have come back after his execution to haunt the place as a black hellhound. Bungay has quite a reputation for being haunted by black hellhounds, to the point that they have adopted the creature as a symbol for their town. It is rumoured that Bungay Church was once attacked by the Devil himself in the form of such a beast and he killed a man.

"In any case, we knew the stories long before we acquired the castle. In fact, it was part of its charm. My father was convinced he could use the legend to encourage people to visit. After we had arrived and began restoring the place, we of course heard the stories again. Many of the locals were only too delighted to regale us with their own accounts of how they had seen a spectral dog roaming the grounds and heard it howling in the dead of night. One elderly gentleman told us his mother had seen the beast the night before she gave birth to him and she had almost drowned him, fearing that he might turn into a demon because of what she had witnessed. His father only just saved him from the ignoble fate.

"Such fables could surely be found in any village or place with such a long history. My late father, much like myself, has never been inclined towards the supernatural. He believed there was a rational cause for everything. The stories, therefore, did not trouble us. The gentleman we installed as a caretaker has never witnessed anything untoward himself and his sleep has never been disturbed by the howling of a hound.

"However, after we put up the fence, we were approached by one of the oldest gentlemen in the village. It is claimed he is almost 100 years old. He stopped the workmen one day when they were putting up the fence, asking them what they were doing. When they explained to him, he sought out my father immediately, who happened to be inside the cottage. This gentleman declared it was a dreadful mistake to put up the fence.

"My father immediately assumed he was going to protest, like all the other residents had, about the land they were used to walking across being denied to them. However, the old gentleman had a different reason for protesting. He told my father that it was dangerous to fence off the land because the Black Shuck which inhabits the castle likes to roam from the property all the way across the county and back again every night. It is something to do with a curse that was supposed to have befallen the original castle owner. In the form of a Shuck, he has to follow a certain route around the county every night.

"This elderly gentleman told us the iron fencing would prevent the Shuck from leaving the site and this would be disastrous. The demon would grow restless, frantic even, and would begin to cause harm to those living in the area. Naturally, my father didn't believe this, but the old man was so convinced of what he was saying that my father didn't have the heart to merely laugh the matter off. He sat him down and talked to him for a while. Asked him where this notion had come from. Apparently, once many years before, attempts had been made to fence off the area due to concerns about its structural integrity. There had been a recent severe storm and there were fears that part of the wall was going to collapse. Fences were put up to prevent people getting hurt. Not long after, there was supposedly a series of tragic events, including a workman being crushed by falling stonework.

"The strange spate of accidents and misfortunes only ended when the fencing was taken down and local opinion held that the demon dog had finally been allowed to roam as he pleased again, and thus he had stopped attacking those around him."

"I imagine your father didn't take much heed of this," Bainbridge said.

"No, he didn't considered it anything more than local hearsay. The sort of thing people come up with when they are sat around on a dark night with the rain howling outside, especially in a place like that, with the reputation it has. He let the old boy have his say, thanked him for his time, and then carried on with his plans. Not long after that, things began to happen. Odd things."

"How odd?" Bainbridge asked.

"The workmen kept finding their tools moved around in the castle grounds overnight. This was after the fence had been put up and the gates locked, therefore it should not be possible for their tools to be moved. Yet, every morning when they arrived, they would find the tools they had carefully put away the night before scattered across the site, causing a delay to starting work. This became quite frustrating.

"It also caused people to talk and wonder if maybe there was some truth to the spirit stories. Workmen can be very superstitious."

"It could just as easily have been something like a fox getting into the toolbox, shifting everything around," Victoria suggested. "Or one of the workmen could have been playing a joke on the others."

"My father came up with similar suggestions, so we ignored the problem. Then other things began to occur. One of the workmen who was there late one evening claimed he saw a shadowy figure right at the very top of the ruins, in a place it is impossible for a person to reach. He was unsettled by the sight, convinced that the figure was staring at him, and he ran all the way home. He returned to work the next day only after his wife convinced him that there was nothing to worry about. But after that he refused to be alone at the site.

"Of course, once one workman starts saying things like that fear swiftly runs through all the others like a plague. They all start to see things. Odd shadows. Black dogs. Everything evil you can imagine.

"Even so, we managed to reach a stage where we could open the place for visitors. The visitors arrived for the first day and everything went smoothly enough. But on the second day, there was a peculiar incident. A child went missing for a full hour. His mother was frantic. When he was finally found and returned, he was asked where he had been. He said that a kindly gentleman in a black cloak had asked if he wanted a tour of the castle, and he had agreed. He had then disappeared off with him for an hour.

"No one knew who the gentleman in the black cloak was. No one else had seen him and the incident raised some eyebrows among everybody there. Before the day was out people were suggesting that it was the castle's phantom the boy had wandered off with."

"Or it could have been simply anyone," Victoria remarked. "The most logical solution is that the boy came across someone wearing a black cloak, who thought he was lost or took a shine to him and wanted to give him a tour. Not to be unkind, but there are a few evil-minded individuals out in the world who would steal a lad given the opportunity."

"Yet the lad was returned unharmed and seemed to have enjoyed his hour's tour of the castle when no one else saw him. It is all rather peculiar. Still that is by the by," Brooksby carried on. "The child was unhurt. The mother was consoled that he had probably just run off and let his imagination get the better of him, and things returned to normal. For a time, there were no further serious incidents. Only minor things that could be explained away as a casual coincidence. The tools of the workmen still kept going missing. Occasionally visitors would report seeing a shadowy figure around the ruins, especially in the evening. Once, a visitor actually managed to get themselves trapped when the gates were locked with them still inside. They claimed they had drifted into another time and only returned after the gates were closed for the day."

"Excuse me, another time?" Victoria asked, raising an eyebrow.

"That is exactly how they phrased it. They said they had been walking around the ruins when they had been suddenly transported to the same place several hundred years in the past. They witnessed the castle being used as a dwelling place; the floors were intact, and a large table stood in one of the rooms. They saw people in the costumes of the Middle Ages and heard them speaking a form of English that sounded archaic to their ears. They had wandered through this scene, apparently unnoticed by those around them, until suddenly the apparition just burst like a bubble, and they found themselves back where they had begun. But now it was several hours later, and the gates had been shut."

"It sounds more like they fell asleep," Bainbridge declared. "I do that all the time."

"You are no doubt correct," Brooksby nodded. "But you know how these stories take hold and people elaborate on them. They refuse to listen to a rational explanation and instead enjoy creating these weird notions of ghostly time slips. It becomes hugely frustrating. On the other hand, it is actually drawing more and more visitors to the grounds."

"At least that is something," Victoria consoled him.

Brooksby nodded his head, before continuing with his story.

"There was nothing else particularly alarming for the rest of the season we were open to visitors. We closed at the end of September intending to carry on our restoration work. As I mentioned earlier, we wanted to place a roof above some of the areas of the castle to make a pleasant seating area in all weathers for the visitors to enjoy. We also had more work intended for the cottage.

"Then, on the 31st of October, there was a terrible storm, thunder, and lightning screeching through the sky. The locals get rather twitchy about storms. It was said it was on the back of such a terrible storm that the Devil struck Bungay church all those centuries ago and killed people within. He supposedly came down on a streak of lightning.

"In any case, the storm wailed around the grounds and the caretaker who usually looks after the place discovered that the house was not as waterproof as he would have liked. When the morning came, we found that the castle had been assaulted by the high winds of the storm and a portion of the walls had fallen down. We postulated the castle might even have been struck by lightning.

Either way, my father felt it was an opportunity to rebuild some of the walls, maybe even to restore the castle to how it once looked, at least in parts. He started to spend all his days going around the castle, trying to determine the best place to begin his plans of renovation. He was making sketches and even summoned an architect to ask his opinion. The architect was mildly concerned that my father's plans were perhaps not historically in keeping with the rest of the castle, but my father had in his mind exactly what he wanted.

"The dreadful accident occurred one day when he was going around the castle ruins. He was planning out how to recreate a scene from mediaeval life within the restored walls and make the castle look whole again when it happened."

Brooksby faltered as he came to the heart of his story; his mind flicked back to his father and the pain of grief surged within him again.

"What exactly happened?" Bainbridge asked.

"My father was at the base of the castle wall in an area where stonework had fallen down previously. He was leaning against the wall, making a sketch of the landscape as he watched the sun rise up over the horizon. He liked to watch the sunrise there. He said it gave amazing views and he often went to the castle long before dawn just so he could watch the sun come up. As you can imagine, he was completely alone, so we don't know precisely what happened. All we know is that after he did not turn up for breakfast, the caretaker, who was used to sharing a cup of tea with him in the mornings, wandered around to see where he was.

"He found him, sure enough, lying on the ground with several large, loose slabs of stone scattered across his body. One of them had slammed down firmly on the top of my father's head. The doctor said he probably died instantly. The obvious conclusion would be that the stonework was looser than we had anticipated, and a terrible tragedy had occurred."

"But you do not think that was the case," Victoria nudged him when he hesitated once more.

"No, neither my mother nor I were convinced that was the case. You see, we spoke to the workmen, and they assured us that particular area of wall was sound, that it should not have fallen. More to the point, the stones that were recovered from the site were not the type that they would have anticipated to have come from the upper wall of the castle. They were large pieces of masonry more suited to the foundations. All this began to raise a question in my mind. What if it wasn't an accident, what if someone had deliberately thrown a stone down upon him?"

"What would the purpose for that be?" Bainbridge asked.

"To stop his plans for the castle? Revenge for him fencing it off?" Brooksby shook his head. "Maybe some other reason I haven't yet determined? I am certain that it wasn't just an accident. Since that day I've been trying to carry on my father's projects. I felt I should do it in his memory. But there have been further odd incidences revolving around myself, which now make me even more concerned."

"What sort of odd incidents?" Bainbridge enquired.

"Well, last night I very nearly died."

Three

Brooksby's statement had caught them a little off guard. It was not only troubling, but deeply disturbing for the gentleman in question, raising even more concerns about what might have happened to his father.

"You need to elaborate further on what happened," Bainbridge told the gentleman. "We need to understand precisely what is going on."

Brooksby sighed before continuing on with his explanation.

"I was at the site late last night. It was already dark, and it had been a long day. We had a new architect visit us to discuss our future plans for the castle. I was not intending to rebuild the walls as my father had, but I fancied we needed to look at putting in some more structural supports to ensure everything was safe for visitors. The architect wanted to undertake a full survey of the site, from the ground up, to determine precisely what needed to be done. This I was agreeable to. So far we had worked mainly on the external portions of the castle, doing very little internally. A full survey would be for the best. We really needed to know what was a priority for repair, and what could be left until a later day.

"I had just agreed with the architect for him to begin conducting the survey next week when he could bring a couple of assistants with him. The evening was drawing on as we shook hands, and he departed. The caretaker was in the process of closing the gates. He asked me if I wanted a cup of tea before I left and I was cold so I decided I would take one. He went inside the cottage to make it, while I took one last stroll around the walls of the castle. As I walked, I was glancing up to note some of the things that the architect had mentioned in the dimming light.

"The architect had gone so far as to suggest it might be feasible to reinstate the floors, so that people could get to the very top of the castle and look out across the landscape. It would be an amazing view, for sure. I found myself wondering just what it would be like to be up that height and looking out for miles and miles.

"It was in that moment, as I was glancing up and the shadows of the evening were drawing deeply around me, that I thought I saw something. It was just for a second. It could have easily been a bird, as it reminded me of the flutter of black wings, but at the same time, I thought it might be the edge of a cloak flapping right at the top of the castle. A place impossible for anyone to get to.

"I put my monocle in my eye as I peered up, trying to see more clearly, what I thought I had witnessed. It was in that instant that I heard a strange, grumbling, crackling noise behind me. Fortunately, my instincts were stronger than my rational mind, for before my brain had even considered it, I jumped out of the way, and thank goodness I did! For a rock came tumbling down, and had I remained where I was, it would have cracked me immediately on the head, just as my father had perished.

"Upon seeing this, I was appalled. I glanced back up to the top of the walls, but could see nothing, and now the darkness was coming on thickly. I was so shaken by events, I raced back into the caretaker's cottage and found him brewing up a pot of tea. I was trembling all over, but I didn't mention to him what had occurred because he has to sleep there overnight. What would be the point in frightening him? I told him I was very cold to explain my shivering and drank my cup of tea as fast as I could before I left.

"All that night, the incident was playing on my mind. I found myself thinking over and over whether it had just been a trick of the light, or had I witnessed someone trying to kill me? I don't believe it was a phantom, of course. I believe there is some mortal person behind this and they're playing on the idea of demon dogs and devils to carry out their crimes. They're trying to scare me away or kill me so I can do nothing else about the castle.

"I had my doubts about my father's death before, but last night confirmed to me that someone is out to get me and my family. What precisely their reasoning is behind that I do not know. That is why I came to you. I need you to look into this. I need you to find out what is going on. I need you to protect me!"

Bainbridge considered all this for a moment.

"Before I undertake this case, there is one thing I wish to suggest. The simplest solution to your issues would be to lock the gates and walk away. Remove the caretaker from the site and leave it as it is. Everyone will then be safe from anyone throwing stones."

"I am not prepared to give my persecutor the satisfaction of forcing me to do that," Brooksby shook his head firmly. "I don't scare easily, nor did my father, and the thought that someone is trying to get me to leave the site angers me. They killed my father, and I will not cease until I have discovered them and brought them to justice. You surely must understand that."

Bainbridge did understand that.

"I am perfectly willing to investigate this matter, but I must advise you to limit how much time you spend at the site while we do so. Let us place ourselves in danger, rather than yourself. You should remain as far removed as possible to avoid tempting this saboteur and potential murderer into trying again."

Brooksby nodded his head.

"I am grateful for your consideration. It's very difficult to talk about these things to people. They assume I am going crazy or have become paranoid and started to believe the very stories I previously said were nonsense."

"We will need to visit the castle," Bainbridge continued. "It might also be necessary for us to remain at the site for some time. Could we be housed in the cottage of your caretaker?"

Victoria tried not to pull a face; the thought of staying in a crumbling cottage that leaked rain through the roof did not appeal to her. Brooksby also had to consider for a moment.

"There is not that much room inside the property, but I believe I could make arrangements for you to stay at the local inn, which would be more suitable."

"That would be much more satisfactory," Victoria said quickly.

Bainbridge had no reason to argue with her on the matter. He was just satisfied to have somewhere nearby to the castle so that they wouldn't have to be constantly travelling. Though Bungay was not that far from Norwich, it was still a long journey, either by carriage or by car, and it would take up far too much of their time to be constantly going back and forth.

"Does that mean you will take on my case?" Lord Brooksby asked. "The impression I got from your housekeeper was that it was not something that would interest you."

"I fear my housekeeper did not fully appreciate the situation," Bainbridge told him. "She was under the impression that you wanted me to seek out a phantom dog."

"Oh dear, I fear I did rather burble on your doorstep to her. But no, this is not about a phantom dog. It is about a very living murderer, someone who killed my father. I want you to find them."

"And that is exactly what we will do. We shall pack up some belongings and meet you in Bungay, say around teatime?"

Bainbridge had glanced at the clock in the drawing room and noted it was now lunchtime. He had no intention of missing a meal, so once they had eaten whatever Mrs Huggins presented to them, they would then pack their belongings and travel by car to the rural town of Bungay.

Lord Brooksby was delighted. He thanked them again for their time, told them that he would make the arrangements at the local inn, and would be glad to see them later on. Then he departed.

"Poor gentleman," Victoria remarked once he was gone. "He has done no real harm to anyone and yet someone appears to be out for his blood."

"The fence was no doubt the start of it," Bainbridge replied, rubbing at his chin. "But there is something more to this than simply locals frustrated they can no longer access the castle freely. What is at the heart of this I am not yet sure."

"Well, hopefully no one attempts to throw any stonework at us while we're visiting," Victoria mused on this matter. "Possibly we should invest in iron helmets to protect ourselves."

Bainbridge was amused at her suggestion.

"I think it will probably be sufficient to simply not go too close to the walls at any point," He declared.

Mrs Huggins fed them well at lunchtime, aware that they were going to be departing from her company for at least a few days. She was always concerned about how well Bainbridge ate when he was no longer under her gaze. When he informed her he was staying at an inn, she pulled a face. She was not convinced that rural cooking was up to her usual standard, but she could hardly argue about it. She compensated by making them far too much food at lunch time, serving soup, sandwiches and pastries that made Victoria frown in consternation.

She was always attempting to moderate her diet to maintain her figure. Bainbridge was not of the same opinion. He was quite happy to eat his fill. Even so, there was food leftover and Mrs Huggins immediately said she would pack it up for them just in case the evening meal at the inn was not up to scratch.

They headed off in Victoria's car. She had acquired the vehicle after she had broken her engagement from Sven, her former fiancé. Technically it had been *his* car, but he had gifted it to her, and she had kept it after his betrayal. She liked being able to drive; it was a novelty for many people to see a car coming along the road, not to mention the sight of a woman driving it.

Victoria did not go particularly fast, and it had been known for her to be overtaken by pedestrians before now. Despite this, she still felt as though she was a modern woman. Now it was the year 1900, she felt even prouder of her car and the fact that she drove it herself.

Bainbridge liked the car because it meant less walking for him. He didn't have his own coach - the expense of keeping it and the horses, along with having someone to drive it, was prohibitive. Before Victoria arrived he had simply walked everywhere. In an emergency, or if he needed to go a long distance, he could always hire a cab. He knew a few of the local cab drivers well enough to get a low rate. But having a car at his disposal was incredibly convenient, did not cost the same as owning horses did, (a car did not have to be fed, you just had to buy the fuel for it every once in a while) and enabled him to undertake more cases.

Halfway along their journey to Bungay, spits of rain started to fall, and Victoria pulled over so she could pull the leather, foldable roof of the car up. Bainbridge watched as she battled to pull out the covering on its stiff hinges and hooked it to the front windscreen. She finished just in time, the heavens opened moments after she was back inside the car and driving off once again.

If Bainbridge had one complaint about cars, it was the fact that no one had considered it advisable to put protective shielding along the sides of them for when it rained. While the roof came up and covered the heads of the passengers, the sides remained open and exposed. There were no doors to prevent rain being blown into the vehicle, only blankets and travelling capes to help protect them.

Bainbridge felt there were still a lot of flaws in car design that needed to be ironed out; you never had to worry about such a thing in a coach.

As they carried on, Victoria only grumbled once or twice about the fact Bainbridge merely watched her put up the roof and didn't assist. Bainbridge held to his theory that if Victoria was a truly independent woman, it would be rude of him to suddenly step in and try to undertake any tasks she was performing. Victoria did not accept this argument with the grace he thought it warranted it, in fact she mumbled something under her breath about 'lazy, old men' which he chose not to hear.

Victoria was determined to reach Bungay before night drew on fully. Though she knew how to light the lamps at the front of the car, she wasn't convinced by their power and hated driving in the dark.

They were soon heading out of Norwich and rolling down rural roads, glancing at the cows in the fields and the occasional horse. A worn roadway marker pointed them in the direction of Bungay, and it was not long before they spotted the first houses of the town coming into view. They were old Elizabethan properties with white plaster and wooden beams. They lined the road in a slightly higgledy piggledy fashion. Some of the roofs were sagging dreadfully in the middle, and more than one house appeared to have its floors tilted at a precarious angle. Bungay was a very old town. There had been a fire several centuries ago, which had destroyed parts of it, but many of its ancient houses remained and harked back to another time.

The car rumbled over cobblestones, bouncing up and down in an unbecoming fashion that jerked Bainbridge in his seat. Locals wandering along the pavements were astonished at the sight of the vehicle juddering along – none of them had ever seen a car before. They paused to watch as the strange contraption bumped across their cobbles, while the lady and gentleman within held onto their hats.

Between trying to keep himself in his seat and stopping his hat from flying away, Bainbridge lifted his arm and pointed to a long, low building with exposed black timbers on its facade.

"I suspect that is the inn," he said, his words jumping about as he was rocked in his seat.

The property had a sign hanging from its frontage that declared it was the *Black Dog Inn*. Painted on the sign was a dark hound-like beast with its hackles raised and a savage glare in its eyes. It seemed to bare its teeth at everybody coming past.

Not exactly the most welcoming of images for an inn.

There was a large archway leading to a courtyard behind the property. Victoria turned off the roadway and bounced along more cobbles, feeling as though her bones were going to be shattered by the motion, and finally found herself behind the inn. There were a couple of horses in the stables to one side of the yard who bucked and reared their heads at the sight of the monstrosity entering their peaceful enclosure. To them the car was a demon that chugged and roared while it puffed out a strange, obnoxious smell.

A stable boy darted out and glared at them, though as much in surprise as anger that they had startled the horses.

"Whoa there!" He yelled at them, waving his hands at them, and trying to stop the car as if it were a runaway horse.

Victoria carefully pressed her foot onto the brake pedal and brought the contraption to an almost graceful halt.

"What do you think you're doing?" The lad demanded, coming towards Bainbridge instead of Victoria.

To his mind, you always spoke to a gentleman first rather than a lady, even if it appeared the lady was in charge of the terrible machine that had just driven into his yard.

"We are here to meet Lord Brooksby," Bainbridge told him calmly. "I believe he has arranged for us to have quarters here for the night. We will of course need somewhere for the car to be stored."

The boy looked at the vehicle in astonishment.

"That's a car?" He asked.

"That's exactly what it is, young man," Bainbridge responded.

The stable boy scratched at his head.

"How does it move? Has it got a steam engine inside?"

"It functions by a different type of fuel altogether," Bainbridge responded. "There is an engine underneath the bonnet."

He leaned around the side of the windscreen and tapped the bonnet with his walking stick to indicate where he meant.

"Well, ain't that a thing," the boy said, looking utterly confused. "But it scared the horses. What am I supposed to do with it?"

"It will be perfectly sufficient to park it under a sheltered corner," Victoria replied. "It does not have to go in the stables or a coach house. In fact, if you point me to somewhere that would not be inconvenient for me to leave it, I shall place it there myself."

Looking even more perplexed by this declaration, the stable boy finally indicated a corner of the courtyard which probably wouldn't be used for a while and where the car could be placed without it being an inconvenience. Victoria very carefully backed the car into the spot. She had been practising at reversing and she was getting an awful lot better, though it wasn't unheard of for her to bump into things occasionally.

Once they were satisfactorily parked, they abandoned the car and headed into the inn. They were greeted by the innkeeper, Mr Savage, who clearly knew more about them than the stable boy did.

"His lordship hoped to be here to meet you, but was inconvenienced," he informed them. "I have your rooms all ready if you would like to see them."

He was bustling them up the staircase before they could say anything and showing them to two adjoining rooms that were both spacious and clean. The beds were old-fashioned with posts at each corner, and the linen had a subtle lavender aroma to it. The mattress itself seemed to have seen better days and was soft but it was certainly serviceable. Victoria approved.

Yes, it was slightly rustic, but it would suit them for the brief time they would be there.

After they had been shown around the rooms, they were directed to the communal bathroom at the end of the landing.

"As you are the only guests we have at this time, you should not have any trouble with anybody else disturbing you," the landlord reassured them.

If he was aware of why they were there, he had not mentioned it, and they decided not to raise the topic. Having settled themselves in their rooms, they headed back downstairs to the taproom at the back of the inn to enjoy a hearty supper and consider the adventure ahead.

Four

"I intend to take a stroll around the castle ruins before bed," Bainbridge informed Victoria as they sat before the fire after dinner.

His belly comfortably full, Bainbridge's thoughts had swung back to the castle ruins and the stories of murderous phantoms.

Victoria could not fathom why he wanted to go out in the pouring rain to traipse around the old, fallen castle walls.

"What could you possibly discover taking a look around them in the depths of the night?"

Victoria motioned to a window and the view outside where the rain was falling down heavily.

"It isn't about discovering anything," Bainbridge reassured her. "It is about proving to others that there is nothing to be afraid. Let people see us walking around, looking at the stones in the dark. Let them see us unafraid of ghosts."

Victoria was not convinced. It was one thing to go around claiming they were not scared of ghosts, another thing to stand out in the rain in the middle of the night, getting slowly drenched while proving it. She wondered exactly to whom they were demonstrating their resolve. But her uncle was not to be dissuaded.

In preparation for their investigation, which Bainbridge had foreseen would require them to be outside a good deal in all weathers, Bainbridge had brought with him a sturdy pair of rubber galoshes and a stout raincoat with a hood. It was the sort of oilskin affair that you might see a fisherman or a dock worker wearing.

Victoria did not have anything to protect her from the elements. Nor had she been advised that it would be a good idea to bring something. All she had was a sturdy umbrella and was feeling a touch aggrieved her uncle had failed to enlighten her about his plans.

Even if she put a thick shawl over her dress, she would not be completely immune to the rain and there was a very good chance any hat she wore would be ruined. Fortunately, Victoria did at least possess a pair of robust walking boots. Being a tad embarrassed to be seen in them (a lady of fashion ought not to wear walking boots under a day gown) she typically endeavoured to keep them hidden beneath her skirts so that no one might notice her unusual footwear. They were extremely practical, if somewhat battered and old. She had acquired them second hand from a pawn shop – her mother would be appalled if she knew.

The soggy, puddle-riddled journey to the castle in the rain was going to test her walking boots to the limit and determine if they were as resilient and waterproof as she hoped. As for her umbrella, looking at the wild weather outside, she doubted it was going to be sufficient and probably would be turned inside out by the wind.

But Bainbridge had made-up his mind, and there would be no changing it. Wrapping up in her warmest things, Victoria begrudgingly followed Bainbridge outside. Since it was not that far to the castle, they agreed to walk rather than try to manoeuvre the car out through the tight archway in the dark. Or, rather, Victoria refused to drive at this hour with only the tiny, candlelit headlights of the car for guidance.

For a brief moment, Bainbridge was put out by this declaration, but he resolved himself to the walk and, in fact, became quite cheerful, telling himself that it served a useful purpose. Walking to the castle in a nonchalant fashion would not only alert people to what they were up to, and hopefully arouse their curiosity, but demonstrate that Bainbridge was not scared of spectres and ghouls. Admittedly it was perhaps the wrong evening for such a demonstration, as there were few people out and about. Those with any sense had disappeared into their houses to get away from the tumbling rain. Those that remained were the unfortunates who either had a task to fulfil that forced them to be outside, or those who had no real home to go to.

No matter, those few souls could be witness to Bainbridge's bravery just as well as anyone else.

Together, Bainbridge and Victoria headed up towards the castle ruins. The gates had been left open for them on Bainbridge's request. Lord Brooksby had been concerned about this, but Bainbridge had insisted, reminding his lordship that it was doubtful anybody would be wandering into the grounds at night with all the talk of malicious phantoms.

Walking through the open gates also gave him an opportunity to see just how alert the gatekeeper was. Would he notice them approaching through his little cottage window? Bainbridge glanced over and saw that there was a light glowing inside one of the rooms presumably from a lamp, since the cottage had neither gas nor electricity to provide it with light. It looked a quaint old place and if anywhere ought to be haunted, it should have been the cottage. The castle ruins next to it were certainly spectacular; set against a backdrop of heavy rain and a flimsy moon pushing its way through the clouds, they looked like the perfect dramatic landscape for a gothic novel.

Just inside the gateway, Victoria came to a sharp halt. She was looking up at the ruins. Bainbridge moved a couple of steps ahead before he noticed.

"What are you thinking?"

"I was thinking the castle is the perfect setting for a ghost story," Victoria remarked. "Every inch of these ruins screams haunted. It is almost too convenient."

"Tomorrow, I want to do some research about the castle and its history, Bainbridge said conversationally. Not that I think it will shed any light on this particular case, more out of curiosity.

Bainbridge impatiently stamped his foot and then began moving forward again, leaving his niece behind. They had brought with them storm lanterns, borrowed from the innkeeper. Bainbridge now set about the difficult task of lighting them in the rain. He muttered a few curses as Victoria tried to help shelter the fragile flame of a match so he might light the wick within the casing of the lamp. When they finally succeeded, they discovered the light from the old lanterns did not illuminate much in this dark landscape where everything seemed to be formed of dense shadows.

Still, it was better than nothing and helped Bainbridge work his way around the ruins of the castle.

Calling the remains of the stone structure a 'castle' was rather generous, Bainbridge reflected as they drew closer. It was really a large, round tower. Perhaps there had been further walls at one point, but as it stood in that moment it was just a circular crumbling mass of stonework, not much wider at the base than the cottage next to it.

The remains of an arched doorway allowed access to the interior of the tower, but there was no trace of the upper wooden floors which had rotted away over the centuries.. Fragments of a staircase running around the inside of the walls could be glimpsed here and there, where the interior stonework had crumbled, but they could not be climbed as a fall of masonry had sealed them off.

Bainbridge stepped inside the tower, making sure he was safely away from the walls to avoid falling stonework, then he held up his lantern and tried to glimpse the ruined interior in its frail light. As far as he could tell, the upper walls should be inaccessible, yet someone had found their way right to the top, where they had balanced precariously to throw stones down and pretend to be a sinister phantom.

If the stairs were impossible to use, what alternatives were there? Certain people could be as nimble as monkeys when they chose to be and if they had enough courage they might be able to climb up the outside walls. But who would do such a thing and for what purpose?

Bainbridge spun around in a slow circle, taking a good look at everything. Truthfully, he had not anticipated learning much here in the dark, he had just fancied standing in the alleged haunted ruins in the middle of a storm. It was both spooky and exciting, and it felt just like the sort of thing Sherlock Holmes would do.

Victoria was stumbling around behind him. She had misjudged where the stonework of the entryway into the tower ended and had caught her skirts upon it, smearing them with water and green lichen. Then she had managed to trip over a smaller piece of rubble that was laid on the ground and had badly stubbed her toe. She was not best pleased when she finally found her way through, especially as she knocked her umbrella on the very top of the doorway. Scowling and politely cursing under her breath, she managed to make her way to stand alongside Bainbridge.

"Are you quite satisfied?"

"You sound put out," Bainbridge remarked, hiding the smile that crossed his lips.

"I am put out. I think this is a fool's errand wandering around a ruined castle at night in a rainstorm. What exactly do you hope to gain?"

Bainbridge held his lantern up a little higher.

"Inspiration," he said solemnly.

Victoria scoffed and kicked at a small pebble that was near her foot. It tumbled away across the base of the tower until it hit against a wall. The noise broke the heavy silence that had seemed to engulf the ruins up until that point. It was as if a spell had been broken and they could hear again the steady patter of the rain and their own breathing.

Suddenly, the ruins felt eerie. Victoria shivered at the thought of someone sneaking around above them, someone who was not entirely human, perhaps. A phantasm of the mind, a spectre of the night, something from a horror story.

Victoria was not one to be easily spooked and generally did not believe in ghosts, but on this occasion she felt a tentative surge of fear rushing through her. Her imagination was summoning up all the legends they had been told about this place; envisioning the phantom Lord of the Manor, who upon his untimely death had turned into a demon dog to stalk these ruins and was cursed to run every night around the county before returning.

Victoria shuddered, and it wasn't just because she was cold.

"We have probably done enough," Bainbridge said, at last noticing that his niece was getting drenched. His own raincoat was proving resilient to the weather, but he was beginning to feel the chill of the night eating into him.

They were turning back to leave when they heard someone moving around at the foot of the ruins. A scrambling noise suggested someone was swiftly heading in their direction, and the winking beam of a small lamp shone light over them. Victoria gave a startled gasp, but

Bainbridge was not concerned that it was the phantom of the ruins.

"Who goes there?" A man's voice carried across the empty space. "This is private land."

"You must be Mr Woolmer," Bainbridge moved forward. "You are the guardian and caretaker of these ruins. Lord Brooksby has hired us to resolve the matter of the phantom who is inconveniencing him and his building work," Bainbridge moved forward towards the shadowy figure of the man.

Victoria followed him cautiously, wondering if the appearance of the gatekeeper was simply innocent, or whether it might be a way of luring them into a position where masonry could be tossed down upon them.

She glanced upward, towards the open roof of the ruins, but she could see no one there.

As Bainbridge drew closer to the gatekeeper, Mr Woolmer lifted up his weak lamp; it cast hardly any light at all and was probably the source of the light they had seen through the cottage window. Now he held it up to shine its glow into Bainbridge's face. Despite the all-encompassing hood of the oilskin Bainbridge wore, Woolmer could make out his appearance and recognised him as an older man, close to his own age. This seemed to console him, especially when he then noted Victoria and realised there was a lady present.

"My lordship did tell me that he was employing some people to find out what was going on here at the ruins," he said to Bainbridge. "I was not expecting you to wander around here at night, however."

"Were you not curious that you were told to leave the gates open?" Bainbridge responded to him.

"My lordship instructed me to leave them open, and so I did. It was not my place to question why," Woolmer shrugged his shoulders. "I thought perhaps he was considering what people had said and wanted to ensure that the demon dog could make its way out into the countryside at night."

"You believe in the demon?" Victoria asked him.

Once again, Woolmer gave an impressive shrug.

"Who is to say what goes on in the dead of night? I just leave those sorts of things alone. I do not care to be troubled by them."

"But you braved the weather and the night shadows to come out and see who we were," Bainbridge pointed out.

"Well, that is my job," Woolmer responded. "Besides, you were carrying lanterns. Can't think of the last time when I heard of a ghost carrying a lantern. Nor one that swore so prettily when it stumbled over a rock."

This last was aimed at Victoria. She said nothing.

"As we have disturbed your peace already, and we are causing you to be stuck out here getting wet, perhaps, Mr Woolmer, we could come into your cottage to warm ourselves through again and discuss what has been going on here?"

Woolmer eyed them suspiciously, then nodded his head. He turned around without another word and led them back towards his cottage. In his haste to rush out and see who was traipsing around the ruins, he had left his front door open and had not even bothered to take a hat with him. He was dripping wet as he showed his guests inside his humble cottage.

The glow of the oil lamp provided a better view of the caretaker now they were indoors, especially when he stood by the fire burning in the kitchen hearth and warmed his cold hands. He was an older fellow of indeterminate age. He could be in his sixth decade like Bainbridge, or he could be considerably older. A life of hard work had left him slightly hunched over and he walked with bent knees. Yet he was spry enough; the sort of old man who becomes almost skeletal in their old age and looks as though they are made of twigs bound together with string, but who retains a remarkable amount of strength and dexterity. He retained a full head of white hair, though his eyes had become somewhat milky, and it was unclear just how much Woolmer could actually see of the world around him. Enough, of course, to stop any intruder who came into the grounds, but maybe not enough to be able to recognise them.

Bainbridge fancied that if a determined intruder confronted Mr Woolmer there would not be much he could do about it. In fact, he seemed an incredibly vulnerable individual to be left here to guard the place.

The kitchen had a tiny range set into the fireplace, Woolmer picked up a kettle and set it on his stove to begin making them a cup of tea.

Victoria and Bainbridge brought in their own storm lanterns which caused the small room to become over-illuminated, exaggerating Mr Woolmer's somewhat haggard appearance. He had quite large eyebrows and the brow bone over his forehead seemed to protrude further than it should. There were liver spots across his forehead and his narrow lips were drawn back in an expression of permanent disapproval. It was hard to say what the fellow might have looked like as a younger man. In his old age, he seemed a caricature of an elderly person.

He turned to them and eyed them suspiciously.

"My lordship told me I had to be as accommodating to you as was possible," his scowl suggested he did not like this idea. "I suppose I ought to offer you a cup of tea."

"That would be merely good manners," Victoria responded.

"And while we're having that cup of tea," Bainbridge smiled, "I rather fancy it would be a good time to talk about the things that have been going on here at the ruins."

Mr Woolmer huffed but said no more. As much as he detested his peace and quiet being disturbed, he recognised that he was not going to get away without having a conversation with the pair of unusual detectives.

Five

Mr Woolmer didn't seem to notice the fact that he was dripping water onto the flagstones of the kitchen floor, nor that his clothes were soaked through. Victoria, however, had noticed that she was drenched. The umbrella had really only taken the edge off the pounding rain and the shawl she had placed across her shoulders had failed to protect her dress underneath. She could feel the dampness of the fabric lingering on her and feared if she sat too close to the hearth, she might find steam begin to rise from her.

In contrast, Bainbridge appeared to be completely dry beneath his oilskin, though he did look somewhat like a beached whale as he moved around in the all-encompassing black cape. He had failed to remove it, and it dripped water onto the kitchen floor in an accompanying rhythm to the droplets of water falling from Mr Woolmer.

Bainbridge was taking a good look around the room while Mr Woolmer watched him uneasily.

"You live here all alone, Mr Woolmer," Bainbridge said.

It was a statement rather than a question.

"There is no one here to live with me," Woolmer shrugged. "I never married, and I have served my lordship all my life. I am very grateful for this position he has granted me."

"A fine position for a man in his dotage. A servant, no less. You have your own cottage. Quite the step up in the world."

Mr Woolmer narrowed his eyes at Bainbridge, unsure how to take this statement.

"How do you like it here?" Bainbridge continued, now moving towards the kitchen window, and looking outside to the ruins that abutted to the cottage.

He could see the curve of the tower wall as it met with the cottage wall.

"I think it is a great honour to be here," Woolmer said carefully. "My lordship has trusted me with a very important task, and I am most honoured. Not many men of my age and position could say that they have a whole cottage to themselves."

"You do not find it lonely?" Victoria asked.

Woolmer's attention had been fixed on Bainbridge, now he swung his head back to look at Victoria.

"No, I do not find it lonely. I find this the perfect place for me. I have never been one for company."

"And you're not concerned about potential trespassers causing trouble?" Victoria persisted.

Mr Woolmer stared at her, as if confused by her words.

"My whole purpose here is to take care of the ruins and to see to it that trespassers are not allowed to interfere with my lordship's plans for this place. I undertook the task fully knowing that I might have to see off intruders from time to time. It does not trouble me."

"That is reassuring to hear," Bainbridge turned from the window and smiled at him.

"And what about the spectral trespassers that concern the people of this town?"

Woolmer shrugged his shoulders in an indifferent fashion, as if it didn't matter to him about whether the trespassers were mortal or spectral.

"I am not one to consider ghosts," he said firmly to Bainbridge. "If I hear a noise outside, I think it is made by a living being, be that a fox, a dog, or a man. I do not go around hunting for ghosts."

"Very sensible, indeed," Bainbridge assured him. "Have you had many problems since you arrived here?"

"None in particular," Woolmer snorted. "When I first took up residence in the cottage, we did used to get some of the younger people in the town trying to sneak into the ruins. They would either drink or bring girls with them and get up to mischief within the secrecy of the walls. They were easy enough to scare away. Once the fence went up, it made life even easier."

"Then you really do have quite a pleasant task in your dotage," Victoria said. "It seems quite a nice retirement occupation, just sitting here and watching the world go by."

Woolmer was unsure if her words were meant to be derogatory or to suggest that he was not doing much work at all. He opted not to say anything, as she was clearly his better, at least in terms of class, and he had been raised to respect his betters – even when they did happen to be nosy, bumbling detectives.

"I am curious about your thoughts on what occurred here recently. In particular, the terrible misfortune that befell your former employer," Bainbridge continued. "I understand that the townsfolk are claiming his death and the other accidents to be something to do with the demon dog supposed to haunt this place. A curse if you will."

"If you wish to hear me concur with them you will be sorely disappointed," Woolmer responded. "I don't believe in curses. I do believe in bad luck."

"It was incredible bad luck that stone falling on the late Lord Brooksby," Victoria said to him.

Mr Woolmer became solemn. There was a genuine look of distress and sadness on his face as he reflected on the demise of his late master.

"It was a terrible accident," he said quietly, his eyes not leaving the edge of the table. "The upper walls of these ruins are unstable. The builders have told me that time after time. Wouldn't take much, they said, for a bad gust of wind to cause a chunk of masonry to tumble down. After all, they've already done that in the past. It was just such a shame my late lordship chose to sit and watch the sunset where he did. But what can you do? Perhaps it was God's will."

"Bad luck, God's will," Bainbridge shrugged his own shoulders. "Whatever you call it, it all seems somewhat of a terrible coincidence to happen at this one place, especially after the late Lord Brooksby had upset so many people with his endeavours here."

"He was perfectly in his rights to put up the fence," Woolmer said sharply. "No one could deny him that. It is private land. It always has been."

"But people do not always see things in that way. They see what is traditional, what has always been. If since time immemorial they have been accustomed to roam freely on this piece of land, it makes no difference to them that in the eyes of the law it is private property. To them it seems that their rights have been stolen away."

Mr Woolmer considered this for a moment.

"Even if they did feel that way, what would that have to do with the terrible accident that befell my late lordship?"

"Really, Mr Woolmer? You fail to see the relevance?" Bainbridge was amused. "What about the other incidents? The sightings of a man in a cloak up atop the ruins, for instance?"

Woolmer tipped his head on one side, giving Bainbridge a hard look as if he were being tested.

"I don't know what that is all about," he said. "I have never seen a cloaked figure in these ruins."

"But your employer has," Victoria pointed out. "Lord Brooksby has said himself that he spotted someone atop the walls and that he felt his own life was in peril from them."

Mr Woolmer just shook his head.

"Phantoms don't go around killing people. They are just ephemeral beings. Not that I believe in them."

"What about someone masquerading as a phantom?" Victoria suggested.

Woolmer stared at her for a moment, his eyes burning deeply into hers.

"How would they get up on the walls?"

That was the tricky part. Neither Victoria nor Bainbridge had an answer for him, and without that answer, how could they convince anyone someone was playacting as this phantom? Maybe it really was just a case of bad luck? A ruined tower with dangerous masonry was just an accident waiting to happen.

The kettle had begun to steam behind him, so Woolmer took it up and poured hot water into a brown, battered teapot, which had seen better days. Despite its chips around the spout and lid, it still served its function satisfactorily.

Outside, the wind had now picked up and rain was being splattered against the windows. They could hear the wind howling around the ruins. Suddenly, it seemed the perfect night for a demon dog to go racing across the countryside. Bainbridge wandered back to the window, his arms behind his back, looking out though he couldn't see much. He could just make out the edge of the tower; a part of him liked to imagine he might see a spectre moving in the shadows.

Naturally, he saw nothing. Just the grass damp from the rain glittering in the twilight.

"Have you suffered any discord with the locals around here because of your position as the gatekeeper?" Victoria was asking Woolmer.

"No one bothers me. I am an innocuous old man. They appreciate I am just doing my job. I wander about the town quite often buying supplies and talking to people. The youngsters can be a bit obnoxious sometimes, but that's young people for you. Seems to me the youth of today do not appreciate their elders, as we did in our youth."

It was the complaint that all old people throughout the generations had made, that the youngsters of today (whenever today was) did not respect them, and that they had been much more respectable to their elders. Whether it was ever a true complaint was debatable.

"No one begrudges the fact you are here keeping them out of the ruins?" Victoria asked as she was handed a cup of tea.

Victoria did not fully believe that there was no discord between Woolmer and the locals. After all, he was the one preventing them getting to the castle.

Mr Woolmer, however, refused to be drawn on the matter.

"No one bothers me," he responded. "I have no concerns. In fact, I have made some good friends here abouts and that suits me well."

There was nothing more they could say. Bainbridge approached the table and took up his chipped teacup. He took a long sip of tea, his moustache getting suitably damp in the process.

"Tell me about the men who are working on the ruins?"

Mr Woolmer was surprised by the question.

"What can I tell you about them? They come in the morning, they go in the late afternoon. They do whatever they have to do around here. I don't have much to do with them. I am not their foreman."

"You have not befriended them, as you have the locals?" Bainbridge remarked.

Woolmer pulled a face.

"It is not my place to befriend them. They're here to do a job."

That was the closest they had come to the suggestion that there might be some trouble between Woolmer and anybody on the site. What exactly that trouble was he refused to say, no matter how they worded their questions.

"Well, this has been delightful, Mr Woolmer, but we must be getting back to our own rooms for the night. We shall wish you adieu. I hope you have a peaceful evening."

Mr Woolmer huffed gruffly, then showed them to the door of his cottage. They traipsed out into the night.

Victoria was barely dry from her last journey through the rain. She put up her umbrella, resigning herself to getting wet once more. Bainbridge seemed to have quite settled into his oilskin attire and she wondered if he would ever stop wearing it. He walked ahead of her, with his storm lantern lighting up the path, looking like some giant penguin stumbling about in the dark. She followed behind. Only once did she stop and turn back to the ruins and, just for a very brief moment, she thought she saw someone there. Not up on the battlements but standing in the doorway at the base of the tower where she had so recently stood. It might have been a trick of the moonlight, an illusion cast by weary eyes and a vivid imagination. The next moment the figure was gone.

She followed her uncle back to the inn and they stumbled through the door, both looking like drowned rats. The innkeeper took one look at them and immediately began fussing around them. He escorted them both through to the taproom at the back of his establishment and promised them a warm cup of tea.

Victoria would have rather gone straight to her room and changed her outfit. But when the landlord brought her a variety of blankets and flannel towels to dry herself with she mellowed. She dabbed at her wet hair and face, wondering what she would look like in the morning and if she would ever be able to comb her hair back into something resembling a respectable hairstyle while she was here without her usual array of grooming tools.

Bainbridge merely discarded his oilskin and galoshes; apart from a slight dampness around the cuffs of his jacket, he seemed perfectly dry and though the innkeeper fussed around him even more than he did around Victoria he did not need it.

Victoria felt somewhat annoyed that her uncle was getting all the attention when she was the one who had clearly suffered the most that evening. She was beginning to note that her feet were cold and had a sneaking suspicion that water had slipped into her walking boots. That would mean her stockings would be wet through. She sighed to herself, all she wanted to do was go to her room, change out of her clothes, and get into bed.

The innkeeper insisted on bringing them not only fresh cups of hot tea but slices of the apple pie his wife had recently baked. This had been warmed through just enough to bring out the flavour without risking burning the mouth. The innkeeper presented the pie to them and informed them that it would make them feel all the better for getting wet. Bainbridge tucked in heartily. Victoria concentrated on trying to dry out her hair. When Bainbridge had finished his portion of apple pie he switched plates with Victoria without even saying a word and began on hers. It was an unspoken agreement between them that when food involved sugary pastry Bainbridge was to help himself to Victoria's portion.

"I assume we achieved something productive out of our little expedition tonight?" Victoria said to her uncle.

"We achieved everything I anticipated we would achieve," Bainbridge responded. "We saw nothing in the ruins to suggest they are haunted, and we startled Mr Woolmer."

"You wanted to startle the caretaker?"

"I did indeed, Vicky. Mr Woolmer is a curiosity. He is on that site at all times, if there was someone there wishing to cause harm and disrupt Brooksby's plans to have the castle renovated and opened up to the public, then why has Mr Woolmer not been targeted? He would be the obvious subject of any sort of campaign. Assaulting the caretaker would cause everybody to pay attention. He's there alone, an easy victim. Yet nothing appears to have occurred to him."

"Nothing that he's prepared to tell us about, at least," Victoria responded.

"And therein lies another matter. Mr Woolmer is very determined to insist that there is no such thing as ghosts at those ruins, and that his late employer was the victim of an unfortunate accident."

"Maybe he is right. Maybe the fact he has not had anything occur to him is because there is nobody there to cause it to occur? What has so far happened is just tragic accidents that have then been misinterpreted by the superstitious locals."

Bainbridge smiled as he forked up every last crumb of the apple pie.

"Supposing this is just paranoia? Lord Brooksby thinks any misfortune that occurs around a crumbling ruin is a deliberate attempt against him and his work," Victoria persisted.

"That would certainly be an easy conclusion to this matter."

"But you do not think that is the case?" Victoria knew her uncle all too well.

"I personally think that there has been one misfortune too many to simply chalk it up to bad luck and old ruins. That castle has stood there for centuries without any masonry falling and hurting someone. Now all of a sudden, in the spate of a year, three incidents have occurred of falling masonry. One of which led to the death of Lord Brooksby. It seems somewhat remarkable, don't you think?"

"It does seem rather coincidental," Victoria nodded. "How do you intend to prove that there is someone behind this, a person who has a grudge against Lord Brooksby and his plans?"

"Well, we have to come at it in two directions. first we have to find a likely suspect, someone who has a reason beyond feeling that their traditions have been ignored to wish harm on Lord Brooksby. Secondly, we have to find out who has an opportunity to do this. There has to be a practical side to this mystery, some way that our assailant is climbing up to the top of that tower to achieve their aim."

Victoria briefly thought about mentioning what she had seen in the entranceway to the tower as they had left. Then changed her mind. What had she seen, really? It had just been a fleeting shadow. Surely it had not been whoever was responsible for the accidents at the tower. Her imagination had been running away with her.

"Tomorrow we must speak with all the workmen to see if any of them can tell us anything else about what is going on at the ruins. There has to be a key to this somewhere. Someone has a scrap of information that will make sense of this all."

"Do you think Mr Woolmer is connected to the crimes?"

Bainbridge considered this for a moment.

"My immediate response would be to say no because he is indebted to Brooksby. He has been given that lovely cottage because of his connection to the family and were he to work against them, he could end up homeless. However, I rule out nothing, for Mr Woolmer is there at all times and, as you quite rightly pointed out, nothing has happened to him. It is convenient that he has never been around when the accidents occur."

"You cannot possibly be suggesting that old man is the one climbing up to the top of the tower and masquerading as a phantom! He surely hasn't got the ability to do something like that."

"Never rule anything out," Bainbridge responded to her. "However, I cannot see any motive for him. No, we still have much to learn about this case, but that can all wait until the morning. Right now I suggest we both get to bed and have a good night's sleep. Tomorrow we're going to be extremely busy."

Six

The next day dawned with tentative sunshine glowing through the window of Victoria's room in the inn. The night before she had stripped off her dress, petticoats, and her stockings, finding the latter utterly ruined, and had then towelled herself off once again. Once wrapped in her warmest night dress and with another shawl around her shoulders she had headed for bed. Victoria had shivered constantly for the first part of the night, until finally her body had amounted enough warmth beneath the covers to allow her to fall into a restless sleep. She had feared she might catch a chill from her escapade but awoke feeling her usual self.

She sat up and looked out the window. The sunlight had a golden hue, and it promised to be a nice winter's day. There was frost on both the inside and outside of the window and a nippiness to the air as she stretched her limbs out from under the bed sheets. Cold but bright; she didn't mind a winter's day like that.

Next door, Bainbridge also awoke to the sunshine. Unlike Victoria, he had gone to bed and fallen asleep almost instantly. But he had awoken in the middle of the night with a bad case of the sniffles. Despite his oilskin coat and solid galoshes, he was the one who had succumbed to the elements, and found himself sitting in bed, sneezing heartily.

Coughing and spluttering, he edged out from under the sheets, found his slippers on the floor and stumbled across the cold room in search of his handkerchief. He located it in the pocket of his coat, and returned to bed, blowing his nose, and feeling groggy.

He was in no rush to get up, and when the maid knocked on the door to make up his fire, he was still in his bed. The girl hurried in, started the fire going and then politely asked him if he would care for some breakfast.

Bainbridge decided that an ample cooked breakfast would certainly cure him of his ailment and agreed, but he still made no effort to move out of his bed.

A short time later, Victoria came to the door of his room, knocked, and popped her head inside. She saw her uncle still in his bed, which surprised her.

"Julius, what is the matter?"

Bainbridge coughed into his handkerchief. He felt puffy around his eyes and flushed. His nose was red, raw from blowing it and all he wanted to do was lay back and fall asleep again.

"It appears the Curse of the Bungay Ruins has caught up with me," He told his niece, pulling a smile onto his face.

"Perhaps going out at night in a rainstorm was not the best idea after all," Victoria folded her arms across her chest and glared at her uncle.

"And yet you appear to be as sound as ever," Bainbridge remarked with a hint of irritation, before succumbing to another coughing fit. "I shall be perfectly fine once I have had some breakfast."

"You shall spend the day in bed," Victoria commanded him. "You are not to leave this room. I shall make sure the landlord has you supplied with tea and all manner of nice things to eat so that you recover swiftly."

"Now Vicky..."

"No arguments. What would Mrs Huggins say if I allowed you to get out of that bed when you are clearly full of a cold? You might end up with pneumonia. No, you have to remain there and recuperate. I am perfectly able to follow up this investigation by myself."

Victoria was gracious enough not to say it aloud, but she was somewhat smug that she was the one who had been drenched the night before and yet had not fallen sick, whereas her uncle, who had flaunted around in his fancy oilskin, had now contracted a dreary cold.

Bainbridge sniffled into his handkerchief. He had to admit he did feel quite poorly. He was a touch feverish, and a headache was threatening. As much as he hated to be missing out on a case, it did seem prudent for him to remain exactly where he was.

"We were going to talk to the workmen today," he reminded his niece. "And Lord Brooksby should be at the ruins, he said he would come as soon as we had arrived and settled in."

"I can handle them all by myself," Victoria responded. "Have no fear. You just need to quietly recuperate."

Bainbridge wanted to grumble; quietly recuperating when there was a mystery afoot was disagreeable, but he had to admit that Victoria had a point.

His mind was made up when the maid then arrived with a hearty breakfast and a pot of tea for him. He started to feel a little better about being confined to bed for the day, knowing the landlord would ensure he was sufficiently provisioned with bacon, eggs, and hot tea.

"Very well, Vicky, I shall allow you to go on your own. But you must report back to me at lunchtime. I cannot go all day without knowing what is happening."

Victoria promised she would return around midday, then headed out to begin her own investigation. She was somewhat elated to realise that she was now a *solo* detective. Until then, she had always investigated cases alongside her uncle and felt a little relegated to being his assistant. Now she was going to show everyone how she could shine on her own and that she was perfectly capable of solving this without her uncle at her side.

She paused just briefly in the main room of the inn to speak to the landlord and ask him to keep an eye on her uncle while she was out before she headed off.

The High Street of Bungay was bustling now the rain had stopped and it was turning into a sunny winter's day. Horses pulling carts trundled by and there was the chatter of voices as people mingled in the street. Though it was icy cold outdoors, and Victoria needed her thickest shawl around her shoulders, once she was moving she warmed up quickly. The beaming sun had enough power to it to make the cold breeze just bearable. She headed directly to the ruins.

The gates were still open, and the workmen had arrived. There was five of them and they were all clustered in a spot near the walls waiting to be assigned their tasks for the day. Victoria noticed that Mr Woolmer was loitering around. He didn't seem to be doing anything in particular, aside from smoking his pipe and glaring from the workmen to the street and back again; he seemed to be waiting for someone.

Victoria surmised that he was expecting Lord Brooksby and was trying to keep an eye on the workmen while waiting for him. Perhaps what he had told her and Bainbridge the night before concerning the workmen was not as truthful as it should have been. Was he worried they were not doing their job properly after all?

Victoria walked through the gates and acknowledged Mr Woolmer with a nod, as he stood just beside the gravel path leading directly up to the ruins. Mr Woolmer responded with his own, reluctant nod, but he kept his distance, as if not inclined to speak to her again.

Victoria strolled across the grass towards the workmen. They ranged in age from the youngest, who was a lad of 16, to the oldest who looked to be in his 50s. One of them, who was probably close to Victoria's age, glanced up suddenly and saw her approaching. He immediately put a broad smile on his face.

Victoria was used to these sorts of reactions from young men. Typically, upon seeing her in her fine dress, they would develop an obsequious manner, offset by a gentle flirtatiousness. Occasionally this eventually descended into pure lechery, but on the whole, they were generally respectful. Victoria, after all, looked to be a lady of fashion, even if she was acutely aware that she was wearing her damp walking boots beneath her dress. Her best efforts to dry them out in front of the fire the night before had achieved little.

As she drew closer to the workmen, their stifled discussions came to an abrupt halt, and they watched her approach in uncomfortable silence until she was right on top of them. It was quite apparent she was going to be the one to start the conversation.

"Miss Bovington," she introduced herself. "I am here on behalf of my uncle, Colonel Bainbridge. He is working for Lord Brooksby, who wants us to find out the cause of the unfortunate accidents that have occurred around the ruins and ensure that future accidents are prevented."

That seemed a fairly discreet way of stating that Lord Brooksby was worried the accidents might have a human hand behind them. She didn't want to mention that he was thinking his father had been murdered just yet.

The oldest of the workmen was a gentleman with a salt and pepper beard cut squarely around his jawline. He had a dignified air to him and though his hair was dotted with grey, and his eyes were starting to become a little rheumy, he still retained a glimmer of the handsome man he had once been. He was broad in the shoulder with thick wrists and strong hands, a man who had worked all his life in the building trade and had gained the muscle to prove it.

"I am Mr Dreary," he introduced himself. "Foreman. Perhaps I can answer all your questions?"

Dreary folded his arms across his chest and his colleagues moved back a fraction unconsciously, as if to give him space. He was an imposing fellow, with a stern manner who clearly took no nonsense.

"I am delighted to meet you," Victoria replied. "I wanted to ask your opinion on what has happened here and to inquire about the workman who was injured on the site?"

Dreary had an uneasy look in his eye, as if he didn't entirely trust her.

"A woman asking questions?" He said, frowning.

"I did not realise that women were deemed incapable of asking questions just as a man would," Victoria smiled back at him. "I find we are just as curious and sharp-witted as any gentleman, perhaps even sharper than some."

There was a slight chuckle at her joke among the workmen, until Dreary's glower silenced them.

"It's not that," Dreary seemed a touch embarrassed that he had sounded so brusque. "I'm just not used to being questioned by a woman in a matter like this."

"Someone has to investigate this matter and unfortunately my uncle is unwell, otherwise he would be here himself. As soon as he has recuperated from his indisposition, he will want to speak to you, but he will be most disappointed if I have not been able to gather information for him simply by the fact of my sex."

Dreary was perplexed by this statement.

"I didn't mean to imply we wouldn't speak to you, just seems slightly odd, that's all."

"Do not worry about odd. I do odd all the time," Victoria smiled. "Now let me begin by asking you what you all make of the stories of there being a phantom at these ruins?"

None of the workmen spoke up. Dreary was going to be their spokesperson and they were happy to defer to him.

"We don't believe in phantoms," Dreary said staunchly. "Bad for business are phantoms."

"I quite agree with you on that front," Victoria nodded. "But you must have some opinion on what has been going on here? After all, so many of the locals are saying that there is a ghost around the ruins causing bother because of the fence you put up around the site."

"I say that is all nonsense spouted by people who are annoyed at what has been going on here," Dreary responded. "The locals don't think this site should be turned into private land, even though that is exactly what it has always been. They don't like the fence. They don't like the fact that his lordship is now asking people to pay to come and see the ruins. They don't like that we're stopping them from drinking within the tower walls. That's all it is."

"Have any of these locals become aggressive over the fact that they can no longer access these ruins? Maybe they have accosted you or your workmen in the past?"

"Nothing of the sort," Dreary answered. "We keep our noses out of their business, and they keep their noses out of ours. We come here early in the morning, we get on with our work and we leave."

"None of you are local, then?" Victoria asked.

"Not to the town. Most of us live further out in the countryside. Near enough that it isn't so bad a walk to get here, but not so close that we're involved with the townsfolk. We can keep our heads down and keep our business to ourselves."

That was not entirely helpful, but perhaps Mr Dreary was right? Perhaps no one in the town had seen any need to upset the workers. After all, they were just doing their job.

"Can you tell me about the workman who was injured by falling masonry?"

"That would be Matt," Dreary shot a look in the direction of the man on his left.

This gentleman was a wiry fellow aged in his mid-thirties. He had a squashed looking face and a broken nose. His mouth tended to droop slightly open, which gave him a somewhat gormless appearance. Victoria could not say if he was a simpleton or just happened to look like one.

"Matt was making sure the tools were all away for the evening. He was placing them where we always put them, inside the ruins, to keep them dry and secure. Then some stones fell down from above and clipped him on the shoulder. They dislocated it, didn't they Matt?"

Matt nodded his head but did not voice a response.

"A dislocated shoulder is a nasty business," Victoria said sympathetically. "It must have hurt terribly. I am sorry to hear that."

"It was even worse when the doctor had to put it back into place," Dreary winced. "Don't think we'll forget those screams anytime soon, will we fellas?"

Matt's colleagues chuckled and laughed along with their foreman, as if the screams from the workman as his shoulder was put back into place had been nothing but a good joke.

"Hurt like hell, miss, so it did," Matt spoke now. His voice was clear as a bell, but there was still that droop to the edge of his mouth. He motioned to his arm and patted the shoulder. "All good now though."

"He had to have it in a sling for a few weeks, but he's fine now,"

Dreary added.

"Did you see anybody around when the accident occurred?" Victoria asked.

Matt shook his head.

"I was looking down, sorting out the tools, making sure they were safe. Must have fallen from above me."

"Have any of you witnessed someone lurking around the ruins in a cloak?" Victoria tried next.

"Sometimes we see people lurking around the site who shouldn't be here," Dreary responded before any of the others could speak. "We've had to chase off a few people in the past."

Victoria sensed that was the most she was going to get from him and the other workmen. She wasn't sure what this silent solidarity was all about. Did they fear Lord Brooksby would think they were spreading rumours of a phantom? Or was it something else? Was Dreary determined to deny a person was sabotaging the ruins to ensure his little workforce didn't panic and depart? What would happen if they were to learn that someone was targeting them on purpose, and that Matt's dislocated shoulder was not just an accident? Would it mean they would put down their tools and stop working?

Victoria tried one last question.

"Do you think the stones that fell on Matt were deliberately thrown at him?"

This question resulted in all five men bursting into laughter. Victoria looked from face to face, trying to see if any of them seemed reluctant in their humour, but they all appeared to be thinking it was a good joke.

"These ruins are dangerous, miss," Dreary told her, now pointing his arm toward the tower behind him. "That's why we're here, after all. The upper levels are all loose stone. It was bound to happen. A pigeon could sit on the wrong stone, flap away and send it tumbling down. We're going to be putting scaffolding up soon so we can reach the upper levels and cement the walls to try and stabilise them before the visitors come again."

"And you are satisfied that is all it was? Badly weathered masonry on the cusp of falling."

"What else would it be?" Dreary shrugged his shoulders.

"I just found myself curious why all of a sudden the masonry would begin to fall when it has sat there for so long. One piece you could understand, but multiple pieces, including the stone that fell fatally on the late Lord Brooksby, does make you wonder."

"Doesn't make me wonder at all," Dreary said dismissively. "We've been doing a lot of work here and that knocks things loose. You see it all the time. You get to a place that's been standing perfectly alright for years, then you start to do bits and pieces, and stuff falls down. It's just the nature of things, nothing to worry about. These old ruins probably would collapse in a few years' time anyway. Just as well we're here to salvage them, isn't that right lads?"

Dreary deliberately looked around at his workmen, encouraging them to join in with his statement. Without hesitation they agreed with him. Victoria was now certain that there was more going on, but Dreary was making sure that no one mentioned it, and there was nothing she could do about that. If he did not want to speak about what was occurring and his men were not going to defy him, then what else could she say? Even Matt didn't seem particularly troubled to remain working in the ruins.

"If that is all miss, we don't have many hours of daylight in the winter. We must be getting on," Dreary ended the conversation.

Victoria sensed that Dreary didn't want to speak to her any longer, so she backed away and let the men go about their work. As she was turning back to where Mr Woolmer had been standing, she noticed that Lord Brooksby's carriage was arriving.

She had a few questions for that gentleman too.

Victoria was determined to find out everything she could about the mystery on her own, even if it meant crawling and climbing around the ruins trying to find out the secrets of the phantom assailant.

Seven

Bainbridge became bored rapidly while sitting in bed with nothing to do. Despite his bad cold, he was beginning to become frustrated with having to rest. The landlord had generously brought him up one of the local newspapers, but it was a couple of days out of date and filled with local information, (such as the price of pigs in the town and news about the recent market days) and it didn't keep him distracted for very long. He was starting to think about getting up and wandering to the castle himself when there was a knock on his door. He called for the person to enter, and it proved to be Mr Savage.

"Sorry to disturb you, Colonel, but I wondered if you might be interested in having a visitor?"

Bainbridge pricked up his ears.

"I am desperately bored; any visitor would be delightful."

"There is a gentleman downstairs who is a local scholar and historian. He's done a lot of research about this town. I thought maybe you'd like to have a chat with him, seeing as you have been so interested in the castle ruins."

"I would like that immensely," Bainbridge assured him.

The landlord nodded and headed back downstairs. A short time later, a gentleman appeared at the door of Bainbridge's room. He was older than Bainbridge, with wispy white hair that wafted around his eyes, but had mostly vanished on the top of his head. On his nose he wore a brass pair of spectacles, and he had a quaint, grandfatherly look about him. He wandered across the room, leaning heavily on a walking stick.

"Mr Hollobone, at your service," the gentleman introduced himself with a stilted bow.

"Colonel Bainbridge," Bainbridge responded. "I am delighted to meet you. The innkeeper informed me that you know a lot about the local history here."

"I do indeed. It has been a passion of mine for many years. I moved here after I retired from teaching at King's College, Cambridge. I welcomed the change of a busy academic life for something quieter, but I could not resist becoming interested in the history of the town. I have written a couple of books on the subject. Nothing dramatic, more pamphlets than anything," Hollobone smiled self-deprecatingly, modest about his achievements. "If you are inclined, I would happily gift you a copy of each."

"I certainly would like to hear all about this town and its curious history."

Bainbridge instructed Hollobone to grab one of the wooden chairs dotted around the small table in the room and position himself near the bed. Hollobone obliged, keeping a respectful distance as he did not want to become acquainted with Bainbridge's cold.

"The innkeeper informed me that you are here because of the recent accidents at the castle ruins?" Hollobone began.

"I imagine you know all about how the late Lord Brooksby wished to turn the castle into a place of education and his unfortunate, untimely death."

"Yes, I know all the details. Along with the stories and rumours that are going about town, people say it is due to the curse of Hugh Fitzhubert."

Bainbridge pricked his ears.

"Who is this Fitzhubert fellow and how does he fit in?"

"I should really refer to him as Baron Fitzhubert. He was the owner of the castle in the days of Edward I and Edward II. He built the structure that you see. It was intended to be his keep and his home, a fortress that he could use to lord it over his entire manor, but Fitzhubert was not the cleverest of fellows. Or rather, he thought himself clever, but in fact was merely devious."

"How intriguing. What did he do?"

"He made the unfortunate decision to side with the nobles who rose up against King Edward II. I presume you are aware of the stories?"

"I do know my history," Bainbridge agreed. "After the death of Edward I, who was by all accounts a strong and iron-willed king, his son Edward II took the throne, but he could not live up to his father's reputation. A series of political misfortunes and failures in battle led to some of his nobles becoming resentful of the Crown and thinking that it would be better for all of England if he were deposed."

Hollobone was nodding his head as Bainbridge spoke.

"Edward II was certainly an unlucky king, though some might argue it was the choices he made that brought down that bad luck upon him. One of those who stood against him was Hugh Fitzhubert. He had in mind that he could do better under a different ruler. I suspect he also had ambitions toward the throne himself. He was distantly related to Edward II, and by a series of complicated political manoeuvrings he could potentially have found himself wearing the crown. It was a long shot, but a man like Fitzhubert was prepared to try for long shots. As it was, things went badly, as we all know. The rebellion didn't succeed, and Edward retained his throne. Fitzhubert decided to do his best to survive the ordeal by throwing himself on the King's mercy. He swore he would always serve and protect him. On this occasion, Edward II was prepared to believe him. At that point, he was rather desperate for followers and Fitzhubert had enviable power and wealth, not to mention he was a powerful knight who would be valuable in battle.

"It might have been said that Edward II's desperation to keep such noblemen by his side was part of his downfall. His father probably would not have tolerated Fitzhubert's betrayal. But Fitzhubert was granted a reprieve and allowed to keep his head. It didn't last, of course. There was to be a further rebellion, and as we all know, Edward II came to a dreadful fate. Supposedly slain with a red-hot poker in some distant castle, or possibly left to rot in a dungeon."

"A terrible fate indeed for anyone, let alone a king," Bainbridge concurred. "But, of course, his son Edward III proved to be a far better ruler than his father."

"Indeed he did, and he could not tolerate what had occurred with Fitzhubert. The rebellion that had been against his father was too much. He turned against many of the nobles who had thrust his father from the throne and enabled him to take the crown himself. Fitzhubert was one of those who was to succumb to his iron might and determination for justice.

Fitzhubert ended up losing his head. His castle was not finished and never would be. No one has ever resided in it. Some say it didn't even have its floors installed at the time of Fitzhubert's demise. The land was taken back by the Crown and retained by them for many generations before it was eventually granted to a member of the local nobility here. The castle itself was left in the state we see to fall to pieces."

"But there is more to the story, of course. There's talk of this demon that everybody speaks about. Fitzhubert turning into a 'black shuck' or hellhound."

"Well, yes. That is the legend that began to circulate not long after Fitzhubert's demise. From my research, I have come to the conclusion that Fitzhubert was not a very pleasant fellow and it wasn't just the king he turned against. He was best described as a warlord. He tried to steal land from his neighbours, and he tormented the people who were beneath him. I suspect they were calling him a demon long before he was executed. I cannot tell you how long after his death the story began to circulate that Fitzhubert had been transformed into a demon dog, or that he had made a deal with the Devil when trying to overthrow Edward II, but as a result, he is now said to haunt the ruins of his castle as a black shuck.

"There are variations of the legend. Some say he lurks around the ruins and the sight of him bodes ill for any who see him for they shall die an unfortunate death soon after. Others say that he has to make a journey every night from the castle, around the boundaries of his former estates, and back again before dawn. I could go on and on about these legends, there are plenty of them in these parts."

"I assume there is a link with the legend of the church that was struck by lightning?"

"Yes, that story actually refers to two churches, Bungay Church and nearby Blythburgh Church. However, that particular legend stems from a later date and it is suspected it was fabricated by a religious gentleman who was trying to claim that certain natural phenomena had occurred in the past to express God's ill will against those of a sinful nature. Or maybe he did it to sell books, because he wrote about the events in an almanac and putting in such lurid tales of demon dogs was bound to sell copies.

"What I know for certain is that a terrible storm struck one night here in Bungay and continued to Blythburgh. The bell tower of the local church was struck by lightning, and it fell down, crushing two of the bell ringers. There may have also been a second lightning strike that ran down the aisle of the church before it grounded. It was a dreadful calamity for those in the church at the time and perhaps, considering the situation and the period, it is no wonder they began to say the devil himself in the form of a demon dog had come racing through the church."

"Which brings us soundly back to the ruins of the castle," Bainbridge nodded. "How easy it would be for someone wishing misfortune on Lord Brooksby to begin pretending to be the ghost of Fitzhubert, scare the locals away, and make it seem as though there was a curse."

"If that is what you choose to believe," Hollobone said. "Personally, I think that whatever is happening in those ruins is a case of bad luck combined with a very old structure on the cusp of falling down."

Bainbridge was intrigued by this statement. So far, most people had been rather too inclined towards the legend of the black shuck and did not want to admit that there could be a rational explanation behind the accidents.

"You do not think someone might be deliberately sabotaging the site and creating these *accidents*?" Bainbridge asked the historian.

Hollobone considered the question for a while.

"I suppose it is possible that someone in the local vicinity doesn't like the idea of the ruins being enclosed to prevent free access to them. Personally, I dislike the idea, as it means if I wish to observe the ruins I must now pay for the privilege."

"There are plenty of people around who think the same and are concerned good grazing land will be lost to them."

"But how many such individuals would go so far as to pretend to be a phantom as you suggest? You would have to be pretty devious to consider doing something like that," Hollobone became thoughtful. "Mind you, they used to tell stories of how smugglers would spread ghost stories to keep people off the streets at night when they were working. Though we are not close to the sea, this town has always had a connection to smuggling."

Bainbridge was intrigued.

"Perhaps you could elaborate on that for me, Mr Hollobone?"

"I'm afraid I only have heard the rumours myself. But I am aware that there are people in this town who are dealing in goods that, shall we say, have not been brought to this country legally. Smuggling, of course, was a rife business all along the coastline of Suffolk and Norfolk in the past. While it's not quite as big a business as it used to be, there are still people inclined to bring goods illegally into the county. They have to hide them somewhere before passing them along. I have long fancied that this town is part of a broader smuggling network. There are certain people here who appear to have, shall we say, a slightly suspicious association with money. They do not appear to work, and yet they always have cash in their pockets."

"That is most interesting, but I don't see how it would fit in with the castle."

"At first glance it would not appear to do so. But you see, this is my thinking, Colonel Bainbridge. I've always supposed that there is more to those castle ruins than what we see."

"I thought you said that Fitzhubert had only just finished the construction of the place before his execution?"

"I did indeed say that," Hollobone smiled to see Bainbridge had been paying attention. "But what sort of castle would it be without some form of dungeon beneath it? Yet no one has ever found the dungeon that ought to be associated with Bungay castle. Even if there was not an actual dungeon as such, the castle should have a basement or cellar area. Most castles have something of that description beneath them to provide storage, and I cannot see Fitzhubert defying tradition. Besides, the sort of man he was, you would suppose that he would be inclined to have a place where he could throw people who he disagreed with."

"A secret dungeon?" Bainbridge considered the idea. It was fascinating for sure, but with the workmen all over the site you would have supposed, if it existed, it would have been found by now.

"I can see you are not inclined to my idea," Hollobone sighed. "What if I were to tell you that while I was doing my research for my book, I came across an old document in the British Museum that dates from the time of Fitzhubert. This document mentions, admittedly rather obliquely, a secret place a person could be hidden in beneath the castle. The exact phrasing was, 'my Lord, Fitzhubert, keeps a place where a person might vanish. A place where someone who he is disinclined towards will simply disappear into and never be seen again until such time as they rise from the pits of hell.'"

"An oblique statement indeed, and perhaps just a rumour or fanciful legend?"

"Except it is believed that this document was written by someone who once worked as steward for Fitzhubert. It is only a partial document, unfortunately, and badly damaged so we cannot be sure, but it convinces me that there once was a dungeon beneath the castle. Where else would there be a secret place where Fitzhubert kept his enemies?"

It was a curious proposal, but Bainbridge was not convinced. The document could have been referring to a lot of places.

"Fitzhubert must have had a house," he said. "A manor where there could have been a basement."

"True, the Fitzhuberts did have a grand estate, and there was once a medieval manor house in the grounds, though that has long gone, and no trace has been found of it. A new house now stands on the site. I have thoroughly researched the history of the medieval manor house, hoping to find the dungeon located there, without any success. I maintain my opinion that if it is true Fitzhubert had a secret prison for holding his enemies, it must have been beneath the castle tower."

"If he did have such a dungeon, I don't suppose it got any use," Bainbridge shrugged. "He died before he could properly move into his tower."

"Yes, and the tower was always intended to be part of a much larger castle. He probably planned to incorporate a fortified manor house into the structure, as was commonly done. If he had not been so quick to betray his king, he might even have lived long enough to see the project completed."

"Then you are proposing that the reason someone might not wish for the ruins to be restored and remodelled is because there is a risk this secret dungeon would be uncovered? Someone might have already found it and be using it to hide smuggled goods."

Hollobone pulled a face.

"When you put it that way, it does sound like a ridiculous series of suppositions. I admit it is farfetched, but if I am right it would explain why someone doesn't want Lord Brooksby to carry on his renovation project. Though it seems far more logical that people are just angry that he has fenced off the land."

"It is certainly an interesting story," Bainbridge replied.

"There are all sorts of stories of secret tunnels around Bungay, you know. In fact, I read only recently that there is supposedly a tunnel that runs from the ruins of the castle to the church itself. I don't personally hold onto that idea. Underground tunnels are incredibly difficult to dig."

"You have certainly given me much to mull over," Bainbridge said. "I don't suppose you know anything about the author who used to reside in the cottage beside the castle?"

Hollobone shook his head.

"She is recent history, and I'm afraid I am more intrigued by the medieval past. However, I can put you in touch with her family if you are interested. I spoke to them on a few occasions when I was researching the castle, as they have a number of documents on the place. Sadly, none of those documents revealed a secret dungeon. Still, I keep investigating, and if you do happen to come across anything while you're looking into the ruins yourself, I would be most delighted to hear about it."

"I shall certainly endeavour to keep you up to date with any discoveries," Bainbridge promised.

"I do hope you feel better soon, Colonel. There are some nasty fevers going around. Do take good care of yourself."

"My niece would never let me hear the end of it if I didn't!"

Hollobone laughed and made his excuses to depart, handing Bainbridge his calling card as he went.

Bainbridge had enjoyed the distraction, but now noted the time was close to midday and he was looking forward to a fever-quashing, sizeable repast from the landlord. Victoria should also return soon to give him an update on their investigation. He looked out the window at the sunshine which no longer cast its pale fingers across the room.

He thought about Hollobone's story of a secret dungeon at the castle. Bainbridge was inclined to dismiss the idea, but it did occur to him that if there *was* a dungeon beneath the castle, its entranceway might be linked to the cottage next door. If that were the case, then surely its former owner would have been aware of it? For that matter, what about Mr Woolmer who now resided in the cottage? Could it be that he knew nothing about this secret hideaway – if it existed?

Might this be the key to the death of the late Lord Brooksby?

Bainbridge nestled back on his pillows. Even when he was sick and in bed, he was managing to find clues for their case.

What a remarkable detective he truly was.

Eight

Lord Brooksby was obviously relieved to see Victoria standing in the middle of the ruins. He descended from his carriage, glanced around, and the second his eyes locked upon her, he smiled and marched enthusiastically towards her. She guessed that her presence gave him the confidence he needed to stride forward and not fear that something was going to fall on his head.

"Good morning, Miss Bovington. You are here early."

"Solving mysteries waits for no man," Victoria responded. "Unfortunately, my uncle will not be joining us today as he has a slight indisposition."

Lord Brooksby looked immediately concerned.

"This is troubling. Did something fall upon him?"

"Nothing of the sort. He merely has a bad cold. No doubt it wasn't assisted by him traipsing around these ruins last night in the rain, but he did so insist on seeing them in the dark. I can assure you, Lord Brooksby, that nothing occurred while we were here other than that we had a cup of tea with Mr Woolmer."

Brooksby did not look entirely convinced by this. He anxiously glanced about the ruins, but they looked innocuous enough at that time in the morning with the fragile sunshine streaming over them and making them seem almost picturesque.

"I am relieved to learn that he is not suffering from any injury," Brooksby said. "Is he quite comfortable in the inn?"

"My uncle makes himself comfortable wherever he goes," Victoria promised him. "He is quite settled and is being well taken care of."

Lord Brooksby was relieved to hear this. He glanced up at the ruins above them.

"You came here all by yourself?"

His tone of voice implied it was the most extraordinary thing that anyone might do, especially when they were of the female persuasion. Victoria was used to this sort of reaction from gentlemen, and she didn't take it to heart. If she did, she would spend all her time being upset by the unfortunate and unthinking comments that regularly spilled out of other people's mouths when around her. Women were not meant to be private detectives, and they were not meant to wander round dangerous ruins all by themselves.

Brooksby was also slightly embarrassed that Victoria was confidently marching around while he had almost hidden in his carriage, having to brace himself to face the castle ruins and any further bad news that might be brought to his attention.

"There was no point hanging around at the inn," Victoria told him. "I know what I am doing, and I shall report back to my uncle once I have sufficient information. For the time being, I want to see this place for myself in the daylight and to try to get a better picture of what is going on here."

Brooksby nodded his head in understanding.

"Have the workmen spoken to you? Do you need me to suggest to them that they must be on their best behaviour?"

As chivalrous as this was, it was slightly patronising both towards the workmen and Victoria.

"I would rather you did not say anything to them. I fear they are already being cautious about what they say to me, and I don't need them being made even more hesitant to talk to me."

Brooksby frowned at her, confused by this statement; he was uncertain why a young lady would not want men to be careful about what they said around her.

"I could just advise them to mind their manners and not swear in front of you?"

"Lord Brooksby, you would be amazed at the amount of men who have sworn in front of me, and *at* me over the last couple of years, and I can assure you I have neither fainted nor melted into a sobbing wreck as a result of their words."

Brooksby's amazement could not have been more dramatic. His face became a picture of bemused incomprehension.

"I will be perfectly fine," Victoria promised him. "What are your plans for today?"

She hoped to distract him from his unease about her talking to the workmen alone. She was concerned he might start to dog her every step in what he considered a politely protective fashion, and she was sure, if he did that, the workmen would say nothing useful to her.

"I really just came to see what was going on and in case you or your uncle needed any assistance from me."

"I require no assistance," Victoria promised him. "Please feel free to go home if you wish or visit my uncle at the inn. I am sure he would welcome some company."

Brooksby looked very agitated at the thought of leaving a young lady all alone in the castle ruins with his workmen. He was not only troubled by the thought that someone might try something dastardly, like throw a stone at her, but young ladies of a certain class should not simply wander around with working men.

It was unseemly.

Brooksby flapped around for a moment, trying to think of a way that he could remain while also not incurring Victoria's displeasure. He had taken heed that she had disliked it when he tried to act chivalrously.

Truthfully, Brooksby did not understand Victoria. She was very different to the other women he had known in his life. He could not imagine any of the women in his usual social circle being happy to wander around ruins talking to workmen on a winter's day; they would much rather be tucked up in a drawing room. Most of them wouldn't even be out of bed at this time of the day.

His consternation only increased when he suddenly noticed Victoria was wearing stout walking boots. This revelation threw him into a new, alarming state of bafflement.

Just what sort of a woman was Victoria Bovington?

Lord Brooksby was out of his depth, and he had no idea how he was going to survive the next few days with this peculiar woman constantly making him revise his thoughts on the fairer sex.

"I think I will just remain here," he said, glancing around him and trying to think of a suitable excuse.

His eyes suddenly latched on to Mr Woolmer, who was loitering around the front of his cottage.

"I need to talk to Mr Woolmer. I shall be in the cottage with him if you need me, and please do not hesitate to come fetch me for anything, anything at all. It need only be a minor inconvenience, but please, I am at your disposal."

Victoria promised him again she would not require his assistance, then wished him a pleasant morning conversing with his caretaker. Brooksby knew when he was being dismissed. He hesitated for a fraction longer, then wandered away to the cottage.

Victoria turned back towards the ruins, her eyes scanning the battlements. She was convinced there had to be a way up to the top of the ruins despite Mr Dreary's casual comments about falling masonry being a regular hazard when restoring ruinous properties.

She decided to take a closer look at the interior of the tower. Maybe that would give her an idea of how someone could be clambering up the walls.

The middle of the tower was quite wide and vast, the walls themselves were several feet thick, which was typical for a structure that might have to survive a heavy siege. The staircase that had once wound up the interior walls was sandwiched in a space between the outer and inner walls.

Victoria carefully walked around the circular interior; it was dotted with grass, but an effort had been made to make it more suited to visitors. Areas had been cleared and gravel laid spread over the top. The places that had not been touched were ones where there was still fallen masonry dotted around. She went to one such pile of masonry and observed that the stones had been resting there in their tumbled state for many years. It was covered in moss and was disappearing into the grass. This was certainly not a recent fall of stone.

The circular interior of the tower proved unremarkable, but she did find an archway which led up to the ruins of the spiral staircase. At one time it would have run up to the very roof. Victoria followed it for as far as she could go, but she could not reach the first floor before the stairs simply disappeared, fallen away to leave an empty patch of air. The very last step she placed her foot on felt loose, and she paused, looking into the darkness just in front of her feet. What had caused the remainder of the staircase to fall down was a mystery, as was when it happened. She doubted this staircase had been in use for centuries.

She headed back down and explored the other side of the gap where the stairs used to run up the wall without learning anything useful.

She moved back into the centre of the tower and looked up. No sign of a cloaked figure lurking around on the battlements. Victoria studied the walls, seeing the old post holes where once the rafters for the upper floors would have been set. Now they were empty and hollow. She thought about Brooksby's plans to restore those floors, to enable people to go right to the top of the tower and take a good view over the town. There was one person, who didn't like the idea of sharing that view.

The upper walls of the tower were in various states of decay; there were quite a few gaps and shadowy alcoves where someone could hide without anybody noticing them. But how were they getting up there in the first place?

The cottage that adjoined the tower had been built centuries after the original construction, from the fallen stones of the tower. It was tall enough that the roof went above the first floor of the tower. Victoria wondered if, at the time the cottage had been built, the tower had had floors and whether it would have been possible to have rapped on the exterior of cottage wall from the first floor of the castle.

Her musings on the construction of the tower would bring her nowhere. Nor had she yet to discover any trace of their cloaked phantom. Once again, she started to walk around the bottom of the tower, looking for anything on the ground that could give her a hint of who the culprit might be. She spied a button lying among the gravel, but it was a fairly ordinary thing that didn't really tell her anything. For that matter, it could have been dropped by one of the workmen.

Every now and again, as she dropped down to glance at the ground, she felt as though eyes were piercing into her back; an itching sensation began between her shoulder blades, and she would suddenly glance upwards toward the very top of the tower. But there was never anybody there, no matter how quickly she turned. It was probably just paranoia.

Having determined that she had thoroughly scoured the base of the tower without finding anything, she decided to try and speak to some of the workmen away from Mr Dreary. She hoped they might be more revealing to her without their foreman looking over their shoulder. In particular, she wanted to speak to Matt, to find out precisely what had happened when he had suffered his horrible accident. Could he really be so nonchalant about what had occurred?

If she had dislocated her shoulder, she fancied she would have trouble laughing it off as a minor mishap.

Victoria walked out of the tower and was about to attempt to track down the workmen on their own when she heard a voice behind her.

"Cooee! Miss! Miss!"

Victoria glanced over her shoulder and spied an older woman in a shawl and bonnet standing at the gates. The woman wasn't quite prepared to cross over the threshold of the gates, which implied she was a townsperson and was uneasy about trespassing on private land, even though the gates were open. She was trying to attract Victoria's attention and waved her hand furiously, beckoning her over.

Victoria obliged, curious as to what the old woman wanted.

She was probably aged somewhere in her sixties, a stout woman with slightly rounded shoulders and a friendly face, shrouded by her tight bonnet.

"Would you be the young lady who came with a gentleman to investigate the ruins and the phantom?" She asked in a dramatic voice.

"I am," Victoria explained.

"Then I must talk to you at once," the old woman grabbed Victoria's arm and pulled her away as fast as she could. "We need to talk about the phantom. I need to tell you what I saw."

Nine

Bainbridge was feeling a little better after lunch, so much so that he decided to get out of bed. Mr Hollobone had been kind enough to fetch him a selection of books that he thought Bainbridge might find useful, comprising of a variety of volumes on the history of the town, some of them written generations ago.

Mr Hollobone had said that if Bainbridge had any further questions for him, he would gladly answer them, before he wished the colonel a swift recovery and left him in peace to read.

Bainbridge's ever-curious mind was whirling around the possibility of hidden tunnels and the connection with the castle. He was eager to see what books Hollobone had brought him.

One of the volumes was *A Concise History of the Barony of Fitzhubert*. It didn't reveal to him much more than what Hollobone had already told him. Supposedly, at his execution, the final Baron Fitzhubert who had brought down such wrath on himself, had grumbled and cursed people as he went to his death, telling them that he would haunt the ruined tower, and should anyone try to own it after him he would come for them. He also declared that should anyone with royal blood ever come into his tower they would be attacked by his spirit and killed. It was the sort of curse that would have worked well on a medieval audience, though Bainbridge was inclined to think it was a later elaboration, probably by the author of the tract he was reading. The odds of Baron Fitzhubert being allowed to speak so furiously from his execution block struck Bainbridge as unlikely.

There was another book on local legends and Bainbridge was soon absorbed learning about the towns extensive collection of supernatural fables; Bungay had everything from phantom horsemen to spectral ladies. More than one of the houses in the town were supposedly haunted, including the inn at which he was currently staying. As he read about a phantom child who was sometimes seen in an upper window of the inn, Bainbridge found himself glancing around the room.

He shook his head to clear such nonsense from his mind. He didn't believe in spectral entities. He did, however, believe in people making up wild tales and using them for dramatic effect or to sell books.

He was picking up another small book, this one a detailed history of the various noble families in the area, when there was a light knock on his door.

"You may enter," he called out.

The innkeeper appeared at the door. Mr Savage was a very gracious and attentive innkeeper. He only had two guests under his charge at the moment, and he was going to make sure they were well looked after. He was also slightly concerned that one of them had fallen ill so swiftly after their arrival, especially as he was aware of Bainbridge's association with Lord Brooksby.

"How are you feeling, Colonel?"

"I believe the hearty breakfast you kindly sent to me, followed by that most delicious luncheon has worked wonders. I am feeling much more myself," Bainbridge assured him.

Unfortunately, that also happened to be the exact moment

he found it necessary to sneeze rather violently and grab for his handkerchief.

"I am delighted to hear you are on the road to recovery," the innkeeper said a touch uncertainly. "Is there anything I might be able to get you to make you more comfortable? Is the fire warm enough? I could always get you some more blankets."

Bainbridge gave this due thought, but he found the fire was sufficient for his needs and he did not require any more blankets. If anything, he was feeling slightly hot.

"I would not mind some more tea," he suggested. "But I think what I would most appreciate, would be for you to sit down and have a chat with me. You are, after all, a man who has lived in this town a lot of years and must know a great deal about its history."

Mr Savage was surprised by this statement. It was indeed true that he had lived in the town all his life, as had his father and grandfather, and he *did* know a good deal about its history, much of it gathered from talking to people in the pub, but he was rarely asked about this knowledge.

"I don't know how much use I will be to you," he said, moving forward and taking a chair at the table where Bainbridge was going through the books.

"I am simply fascinated by the many legends and stories that are associated with your town. I don't think I've ever been to such a place which has quite the collection of paranormal and legendary stories."

"We do seem to be well stocked in that regard," Mr Savage grinned. "Perhaps it is the case that once you have one good legend, it attracts others?"

"Perhaps you are right, Mr Savage. May I ask, are you a believer in the supernatural or a sceptic?"

Mr Savage considered this for a moment.

"I do not think, Colonel, that I could attribute myself to either category. On the one hand, I am fairly cynical about a lot of the stories I hear. Told to me usually by a drunkard who has come in from a wild night and been spooked by something. I don't believe, for instance, that a phantom highwayman rides up and down the main High Street every night. After all, I am here at all hours and my inn stands right on the High Street, yet I have never seen him. However, there are other things that do make me wonder. After all, I am a church-going gentleman, and if one believes in God and the angels, then surely one must have to consider there could be other things out there of a spiritual nature?"

"A very wise statement," Bainbridge concurred. "You are correct that as a God-fearing nation we must consider that there are other things out there. After all, in the past, people were far more prepared to talk of visits by angels and visions. Monks were quite renowned for it."

"Sometimes I think, with the way we have become so industrialised, we have forgotten that part of ourselves. We are so caught up with science and machines. We think there is an answer to everything. Everything has a solution. You can make anything happen, just with the right mechanics. I rather feel that is a very dull way of looking upon the world. Maybe even a sad way. I like the idea that there is still a little magic left."

"You and me both, Mr Savage," Bainbridge smiled in agreement. "May I ask, therefore, where you stand in regard to this phantom haunting the castle ruins?"

"That is, indeed, a curious story," Mr Savage began. "Over the years I have run this inn, I have heard about many encounters with that particular phantom. Admittedly, not all of them come from terribly reliable sources, but I have seen people come in here, their faces white as sheets, saying they have just seen a demon dog race out from the tower and dart past them, or a lonely figure in a cloak right on the very top of the tower. And these were people who I would argue were sensible and sober. Not the sort to come up with wild tales."

"What do you make of their stories, then?" Bainbridge asked.

"Well, if I were to look at them purely rationally, I could argue that any old dog could run away from the tower ruins and if it happened to be of a dark colour and raced past a person then it would be easy enough for them to surmise they had seen a demon dog. That would account for the situation. After all, there are plenty of dogs in the town, and I know of more than one person who allows their dog to run around on the tower green, or at least they did before the fence was put up."

"Yes, a regular stray dog, or even one that was not a stray, would certainly account for that situation," Bainbridge agreed. "For that matter, some people, in the right frame of mind would be spooked enough by seeing a large fox and assume it was a demon dog if the shadows were just right."

"That is precisely it. I don't think any of these people who told me this story were lying. Some of them were very respectable; one was even a lady. I think misguided might be the word I would use to interpret their stories."

Bainbridge thought that was a very logical argument and was pleased to see that Mr Savage was a sensible individual who did not take to heart all the rambling stories his customers told him.

"I have a feeling you are going to tell me there is more to your view on the subject than simply people mistaking a local dog for a demon?" Bainbridge said.

"You are correct. As much as I like to find a rational explanation for everything, there are occasions when a story comes to my ears, and I have to wonder about it. Not so much the demon dog, but the stories about a gentleman cloaked all in black, wandering around the ruins. For instance, there was one elderly lady who stumbled into my inn one night talking about seeing the figure. Now, she was a teetotaller, so to see her stumbling into my inn was quite a shock, not just to me, but to everybody there. We don't typically allow women in the front room, unless of course they're guests heading upstairs to the rooms. I was about to suggest that she must have stumbled into the wrong place, perhaps looking for a neighbour's house, when I saw the expression on her face.

"The horror on her features told me everything. In fact, I was quite alarmed and thought she might faint. My wife wondered if she was having an apoplectic fit. We quickly ushered her into a chair. She could barely speak, just mumbling words. We were close to calling the doctor when she finally found her voice and explained how she had been heading for home after a long day at the market. She happened to be walking past the tower – when I say walking past, I mean she was literally cutting across the grass beside the tower. She was at the base of the tower when something caused her to glance upwards. That's when she saw a man, dressed all in black, a hood up over his head. She couldn't see a face or arms, just his shape silhouetted against the setting sun. He was staring down directly at her.

"He stood atop the tower wall where no one could climb and he was leering at her, though how she could tell with the hood covering his face is debatable, but that was the feeling she got. He radiated malevolence and she was alarmed. She blinked her eyes for a moment, thinking she was delusional, even took off her glasses to rub at them, and when she looked up again, he was gone. Simply vanished into thin air. That was when she started to panic. She raced to the nearest place of safety, which happened to be my inn.

"It took a good deal of consoling to calm her nerves. She was convinced it was an omen of her death soon to come. It is said that if you see either the demon dog or the black phantom on the ruined tower your death will come within a year and a day. I couldn't tell you the basis of that legend, or how many people have succumbed to it, but I will tell you this – the lady in question passed away within the next six months. It was natural causes as she had a bad heart. But the point was she saw that demon figure before she died."

"No doubt such a story would add plenty of fuel to the rumours about Baron Fitzhubert haunting his old tower," Bainbridge mused.

Mr Savage smiled at Bainbridge and nodded his head.

"You truly appreciate how people's minds work. Yes, exactly. I know plenty of people who have claimed to have seen the demon dog or the phantom over the years who are still going strong, but that one story from this particular, respected lady and the fact that she passed away within the six months is all some people need to convince them the legends are true. I know of people who walk past the ruins with a hand to the side of their head to prevent them from accidentally catching a glimpse of the phantom."

"Such an incident is the perfect way to stoke the fires of a legend. But what do you make of it, Mr Savage? What do you feel was going on with the lady you met?"

"Truthfully, I do not know," Mr Savage replied. "She was an honest woman, someone who did not see things, and until that moment I would have argued she had never seen a ghost in her life, nor believed in them. But she was truly upset by something."

"And, of course, all this recent activity at the tower and the death of the late Lord Brooksby are only adding further fuel to the fire."

"That is all anybody talks about," Savage nodded. "They sit at the bar for hours on end debating how the Brooksbys brought this all on themselves. How they never should have tried to fence off the ruins or begun repairing them."

"So people feel that if they had left things alone, then none of this would have happened?"

"Precisely. There was a lady who lived in the cottage that abuts the tower ruins. She didn't live there a lot. In fact, I don't believe she ever stayed overnight at the property, but she would go there during the day. She was a poet or something, I believe. Her name was Ethel Ward, and she never had any bother while she was there. People say that is because she respected the ruins. She didn't try to interfere with them. She just kept herself to herself, used the cottage as her writing retreat and left the phantoms of the night to get on with their own business."

"She sounds like a sensible woman," Bainbridge smiled. "Maybe that was what Lord Brooksby should have done. Then again, what he is doing is not a particularly terrible thing. He wants to encourage people to recognise the ruins for their significance and to salvage them for future generations. If they were purely ignored, they would rot to nothing and then there would be no trace left of the Baron Fitzhubert and his ignominious demise."

"Some I have heard argue that that would be the best way of things," Savage said knowingly. "They don't think you should tamper with the dead and their wishes."

"That sounds very superstitious to me. Not my kettle of fish at all. I must point out, Mr Savage, that I am firmly of the belief that whoever is causing the trouble at the tower is a living, breathing person."

"That is simply preposterous!" Savage almost laughed at this statement, then remembered himself. "No living person could get up onto the top of those tower ruins."

"I keep hearing people say that, but what makes you so sure about it? The ruins themselves are perfectly climbable if one has the courage and the agility. For that matter, we don't know if there might be a secret way up onto them. It seems to me that everybody keeps saying that no one could go up to the tops of the tower simply because they couldn't, not because someone with the right skills could not."

Savage considered this idea.

"But that's preposterous. People have been saying there is a phantom for generations. I remember my grandfather telling me a story about it when I was just a boy."

"I am not suggesting that the legend connected to the tower is not extremely old. What I am merely hinting at is the possibility that whoever our culprit is, is using that legend as a cover for their own nefarious activities. That means not only are they trying to sabotage Lord Brooksby's plans, but that they are directly responsible for the death of his father. It makes them a murderer."

Mr Savage's eyes grew wide at this statement. The thought that the late Lord Brooksby had died at the hands of an irate phantom had seemed somehow inevitable. To suppose he had been killed by a real-life murderer made the whole thing far more horrid. It meant there was someone among them who had decided to end the life of Lord Brooksby. A phantom murderer was somehow easier to forgive and forget about than a real life one.

"The question I find myself asking is *why*?" Bainbridge persisted. "Who would be so angry and agitated about what the late Lord Brooksby was doing that he would begin these acts of sabotage and assassination? Who would risk climbing up to those tower ruins time and time again, placing their own lives in danger, simply to stop the progress of the building work? And why? Can you offer me any suggestions?

Savage shook his head.

"No," he admitted. "I can't think of any reason why someone

would wish to do that."

It seemed a genuine statement.

"Well, if you come across anyone who might be responsible. You must let me know," Bainbridge replied. "You will hear things that I do not."

"If I hear anything of that sort, I will tell you at once," Savage promised him. "But I honestly can't believe that anybody would be going out of their way to hurt the Brooksby family. They have always been good benefactors to the town. They own a lot of land around here. Even though they do not live close by, they have always had an interest in the area."

"Well, someone doesn't agree with their interest," Bainbridge said solemnly. "And that someone has a very nasty way of showing their disapproval."

Ten

The old woman hurried Victoria down a series of winding streets until they came to a small cottage. By the looks of it, it had been around almost as long as the tower itself. Its walls sagged in an ominous fashion, and its windows sloped at a dramatic angle. The old lady showed Victoria into her front room, which was a humble space, crowded with various sizes and shapes of wicker baskets, some of them still in the process of being woven. The lady had to move a few of these items off a chair to give Victoria space to sit down. She looked mildly ashamed that her home was crammed with baskets, though they were clearly her livelihood. Victoria was not concerned.

"You are a basket maker," she said, picking the basket nearest her and admiring its workmanship.

The basket was neatly constructed in tight coils and had been stained to increase its durability.

"I am indeed," the woman said shyly. "My husband taught me the art. After his passing, I kept on his work. It pays well. People are always looking for baskets. I'm trying to expand into things such as straw hats to have more items to sell."

"Your work is admirable," Victoria nodded, running her fingers along the edge of the basket she was holding. It was a large shopping basket that would hang comfortably over a person's arm. Spontaneously, Victoria decided she wanted to buy it.

"I have been in need of a new shopping basket for quite some time but have not found one quite so nice as this. I would very much like to purchase this one."

The old lady looked surprised at this statement.

"If it is not for sale, I fully understand," Victoria hastened to add, thinking she had said something wrong.

"Oh no, I mean, yes, you can certainly purchase that one," the woman responded swiftly. "I was just not expecting you to ask to buy one, seeing as I invited you in."

Victoria drew out her purse and they discussed for a moment how much the basket was worth. The old lady was definitely underselling herself when she named its price, so Victoria added a bit extra to the quantity and refused to take any back.

"It is worth every penny I gave you," she said staunchly, before putting her purse away in a pointed fashion.

The old woman was now both abashed but also cheered that Victoria had put such value onto her craftmanship.

"Would you like a cup of tea?" She said, remembering her manners.

The next few minutes were taken up with the process of boiling the kettle and filling the teapot. Victoria had learned from her uncle that it was always polite to agree to a cup of tea when someone who wanted to speak with you offered it. Bainbridge believed the act of making and drinking tea was both soothing and set the mood for people to be talkative. Speaking over a cup of tea was somehow reassuring, comfortable, normal. It tended to help people open up.

Victoria had originally thought that this was just her uncle's excuse for expecting a cup of tea wherever he went, now she was beginning to appreciate what he had meant. Tea was very conducive to conversation.

Once the teacups were on the table, the elderly basket weaver sat down opposite Victoria and smiled at her.

"I am Mrs Nantwich," she introduced herself.

"Victoria Bovington," Victoria responded.

"I have been hearing talk about your arrival. Everybody was speaking about it in the marketplace earlier today. I was buying up some more reeds to make my baskets with, and all that I could hear people saying was how a gentleman detective and his niece had arrived in town to investigate the mysterious phantom at the tower ruins."

"I had not realised our arrival was already so talked about," Victoria smiled, slightly embarrassed.

"I knew I had to talk to you at once," Mrs Nantwich continued. "I imagine you want to hear any sort of information you can get hold of about the phantom?"

"Yes, and also, no," Victoria responded. "I must point out immediately, Mrs Nantwich, that my uncle and I firmly believe that there is no such thing as a phantom. Whoever is causing trouble at the tower is a living, breathing person who is using the legends to mask their actions and keep people away from the tower."

Victoria had anticipated her statement would disappoint Mrs Nantwich. Instead, she was surprised when the woman nodded at her and smiled.

"I am relieved to hear you say that. People in these parts are very quick to believe in ghosts. All you have to do is look outside my window and you can just see the weathervane in the marketplace, which has a demon dog on the top of it. This place is rife with superstitions and ghost stories; that does not mean that everything that goes bump in the night is a ghost."

Now Victoria was intrigued. She had assumed the woman had

pulled her away from the castle to tell her further stories about the phantom and warn her to stay away. Instead, it seemed that Mrs Nantwich might possess some genuinely useful information about the tower mystery.

"I have been spending time around the tower since I was a little girl," Mrs Nantwich continued. "My father used to always walk us children past it to get to the church. He liked to tell us the story of Baron Fitzhubert as a moral lesson. How one must be loyal to a cause and not simply change sides to seek the best advancement. It was a story that stuck with me. He used to tell us the legends of the demon dog and the phantom too. But I never ever saw any ghost, nor did any of my siblings. I knew people who said they had seen the phantom, but I have walked right past that tower most nights for as long as I can remember, until the fencing went up around it. It was my regular route home. I have walked there in stormy weather and in sunshine, in rain and snow, and I have never encountered anything."

"I get the impression, Mrs Nantwich, that you do not believe in ghosts."

"I believe there is something on the other side of this life," Mrs Nantwich said quietly. "At least I hope so, as I wish to be reunited with my husband when my own time comes. But no, I don't believe in phantoms that haunt the living and stalk around ruined towers. I knew the dear lady writer, Ethel Ward, who used to own the cottage beside the tower."

"I have heard about her," Victoria nodded.

"I used to run chores for her when she was in residence, seeing as I didn't live terribly far from the tower. It suited me to have an extra little bit of income. She was always fascinated by the story of the tower and wanted to write a romantic novel about it. I spent many hours there with her at the cottage. Sometimes, especially in the winter when the afternoons were dark and the wind howled, we talk about the legends. Mrs Ward had never, ever seen anything to convince her that there was a spectre about the place."

"I do not suppose she would care to be there alone at night if she thought the place haunted."

"There was one thing about Mrs Ward that was slightly curious," Mrs Nantwich continued. "No matter how late into the evening she remained at that cottage, she never ever slept there. I once asked her about it. Why travel home in the dark, in all manner of bad weather, when she could have a small bed put upstairs in the perfectly acceptable bedroom? She rode a bicycle, in her later years, though when she first purchased the cottage she always travelled there on horseback. I used to worry about her riding home in the dark, along those lonely country roads. It seemed to me ridiculous that she didn't save herself that bother, and the potential hazards, by simply spending the night in her own cottage. But she told me she could not sleep in that property without explaining to me why."

"That is curious. If she did not believe in spectres, what could possibly prevent her from sleeping in her own property overnight?"

"It was a matter that troubled me for a long time," Mrs Nantwich explained. "Perhaps troubled is not the correct term, it was something that crossed my mind from time to time and that I used to think about. I even discussed it with my late husband. He said perhaps she was one of these people who simply could not sleep alone in the house, that she needed to be home with her husband for company. There are people like that. Or maybe, she did not like sleeping in a strange bed? People can have all sorts of odd fancies, especially when they have the money to indulge them."

"Why are you telling me all this, Mrs Nantwich?" Victoria asked.

"For a couple of reasons, firstly, to impress upon you how often I have been past that tower late at night without anything disturbing me. And the same applies to Mrs Ward, never in all the years I knew her – and it must have been a couple of decades at least – did she ever mention anything about seeing ghosts.

"Secondly, however, I firmly believe that Mrs Ward was a woman of secrets. I always felt there was something not quite right about that cottage and her presence there. It wasn't just that she refused to sleep in the bedroom upstairs, she refused to let me go upstairs at all. I never went beyond the ground floor of that cottage. Every now and again I would ask her if she would like me to dust the bedrooms upstairs, open the windows to air the place out, and give everything a spring clean. I knew those rooms were furnished because I could see the furniture through the windows.

"She always turned me down. Yet she must have gone up there herself, because sometimes I would see the upstairs windows were open. It seemed to me remarkable that she employed me to keep her cottage clean yet wouldn't allow me to ever go up to the first floor. That made me wonder, along with the fact she would never sleep at the cottage, if there was something she was keeping secret."

"Maybe she didn't want to take advantage of your kindness?" Victoria suggested.

"In my experience, people who employ housekeepers and cleaners do not think like that," Mrs Nantwich said politely to Victoria. "As much as I cared about Mrs Ward, I do not believe she was the sort of woman who gave that much thought to those people she employed. We could not be considered friends. She liked to talk to me and sometimes we discussed ideas for her new books. But there was no true friendship. I would not want you to think that that is what I am suggesting. We remained employer and employee."

"But you cannot think of any reason that she would not want you to go to the upper floor of the cottage?"

"That's not quite true. Over the years I've come up with numerous reasons," Mrs Nantwich explained. "I just had no proof for any of them. I was sure she went upstairs from time to time. I saw movement in the upstairs windows and the curtains were always closed at night. She must have been going up and closing them before she left. I did wonder if perhaps she kept important documents related to her books up there, or maybe she had a library. She was very interested in history and collected a lot of old books, which she told me were both valuable and fragile. Maybe that was where she stored them, and she simply didn't want someone accidentally damaging them."

Mrs Nantwich frowned.

"Call it an old woman's fancy, but I always felt there was something more sinister to the whole situation than any of my explanations suggest. I just can't put my finger on what was really happening."

"Now Mrs Ward has passed on, Mr Woolmer must be using those upstairs rooms," Victoria commented. "He doesn't seem to have any issue with the upper floors of the cottage."

"Then all I can say is that whatever Mrs Ward kept up there must have been removed when she died. Or maybe it was nothing more than my fantastical imaginings. I'm sorry if this seems preposterous to you and meaningless. I hoped it might help to share my concerns."

"It does help," Victoria promised her. "I'm just not sure how yet."

This satisfied Mrs Nantwich, though there was still something on her mind.

"Going back to what I told you before, how for all my life I have never seen anything supernatural at the tower. No phantom figures or dogs. That statement was completely true..." Mrs Nantwich hesitated. "Until just recently, that is. Just after the fencing was put up around the tower, and building work began in earnest around the site, things changed."

Mrs Nantwich anxiously stared into her empty teacup.

"For the first time in my life, I saw something there. It was not long after the fence had been put up, and there was a lot of talk around the town, people were upset, saying that the Brooksbys had no right to do that. It was our tower, not theirs. Of course, the Brooksbys had told us that legally they were perfectly allowed to put a fence around the site. They even dared to say it was for safety reasons in case anything fell from the tower battlements.

"Well, none of us had ever seen any masonry fall from that tower. No one had ever been hurt around the site. But after they said about stones falling, it was as if they talked it up. People started to claim they had seen stones just plummet from the battlements, as if pushed by something invisible.

"Everyone was feeling very upset with the Brooksbys. I had to change my route to get home. More than once, as I was walking around the tower on the far side of the metal fence, I found myself glancing at the ruins. I had looked at that tower everyday throughout the years and never had I seen anything apart from some birds roosting on the top.

"But on two different occasions in the last few months, I have seen someone stood up there, silhouetted either by moonlight or the sunset. A figure in a cloak with the hood all the way up over their face, just standing staring out, not in my direction, but looking out over the town. That figure seemed to me as real as you are right now."

Mrs Nantwich paused to considered what she had said.

"Do you see my point? It wasn't until after the fence went up I began to see the supposed phantom. Now, I am a rational woman and after spending so much time around that place and seeing nothing, it occurs to me that putting up the fence was the trigger for it. Whether you believe it's a spectre or a person, you have to agree the two things have to be linked, don't they?"

"Yes, I think they are most definitely linked," Victoria agreed with her. "Someone is trying to disrupt the work that the late Lord Brooksby began. Someone who I think is very, very dangerous."

Mrs Nantwich fumbled with her teacup.

"I don't know what drove me to speak to you today, aside from I felt that maybe you would be interested in my story about Mrs Ward's peculiarities. I don't know if they mean anything but, from one woman to another, do be extremely careful. Whoever is at that tower, they are malicious, and they want to cause harm."

"You don't think it was an accident that the late Lord Brooksby was struck by falling masonry?"

"I believe someone, be they a supernatural entreaty or a regular person, made a deliberate attempt to kill Lord Brooksby and succeeded," Mrs Nantwich took in a deep breath as her anxiety grew with her statement. "And that troubles me deeply, especially when I start to consider Mrs Ward's determination never to remain there overnight. I start to think maybe there's a piece to this puzzle that I have missed all these years. Something I didn't understand. I don't mean to scare you, Miss Bovington. I just want to warn you."

"I am fully alert to the possibility of danger at the site," Victoria promised her. "I won't allow my guard to drop. I will find the truth behind all this. I don't think random pieces of masonry are falling down because of the new restoration work. I think someone is deliberately targeting the workmen and the Brooksbys in an effort to stop them continuing work on the tower. The real question is why? Is it purely due to outrage because the Brooksbys have fenced off the property?"

"All I will say is people around here are quite precious about their heritage," Mrs Nantwich gave a polite shrug of her shoulders. "The tower, the demon dog, even Baron Fitzhubert, are all part of our town's identity and people don't like the thought of losing that. People can be very defensive when they see the old ways and their history being destroyed."

"It is not the intention of Lord Brooksby to destroy your history," Victoria pointed out, though the instant she said it she recalled the late Lord Brooksby's plans of turning the tower into a fantastical, modern interpretation of a medieval castle while paying little heed to historical accuracy.

"Just as long as you take good care of yourself and watch out for..." Mrs Nantwich did not have a chance to finish her statement, because just at that moment pounding feet raced down the road outside her window.

Someone was shouting for a doctor to come urgently. The cry immediately drew their attention.

Victoria rose and went to the door of the cottage, followed by Mrs Nantwich. She could now see the man who was racing down the street calling for help and recognised him even from the back view.

"I believe that is one of the workmen from the tower. Matt, I think his name is."

"Matt Hemsby," Mrs Nantwich responded. "Yes, that's him. I know him from the way he runs. Why is he seeking out a doctor?"

"Something must have happened at the tower," Victoria finished her sentence with her chest filling with mounting horror. "Another accident, perhaps? Oh, my word! If he's rushing like that, it must be serious."

Saying no more, both she and Mrs Nantwich began hurrying towards the tower, hoping beyond hope their worst fears were unfounded – that the phantom had struck again.

Eleven

Lord Brooksby was beside himself when Victoria hastened through the gates towards the tower. Mrs Nantwich lingered a little longer in the entranceway, not entirely convinced she wanted to go towards the foot of the tower.

Victoria had no such qualms. She raced up to his lordship.

"What has happened?"

Lord Brooksby looked pale, a film of sweat dotting his forehead despite the cold day, and his hands trembling.

"Another terrible accident, Miss Bovington. One of the workmen, yet again. Sadly, he was struck on the head. I am not sure he will survive."

Victoria's mouth went dry at the statement. She thought of the gentlemen she had recently spoken to; how they all smiled at her cheerily and dismissed her concerns about a phantom.

How Mr Dreary had refused to hear any talk about a ghost.

It could be no more than a few hours ago they had that conversation, and now one of them was flat on the ground, perhaps dying.

"Show me to him at once, Lord Brooksby," Victoria commanded.

His lordship immediately hesitated. The thought of escorting a young woman to where a man had been badly bashed on the head with a stone filled him with a sense of dread.

"There is a lot of blood, young lady."

"Blood does not cause me any qualms," Victoria said, slightly inaccurately.

"You are more robust than I am," Lord Brooksby sighed. "I hate the sight of blood. I hate to see people hurt. But if you must see him, then you ought to come this way."

Victoria only half heard what he said; she had spied Mr Woolmer standing in his cottage doorway, making no move to see what was going on. She thought that was rather cowardly on his part.

Lord Brooksby escorted her around the curve of the tower wall, they had to walk several paces before they came to the spot where the workmen had been active that day. Lying on the ground, just near a large fallen block of masonry, was one of the younger members of the team. Victoria felt her heart sink as she saw him. His skull had been badly crushed by the falling stone. There was a lot of blood, and he was unconscious. From the looks of the impact, Victoria did not give him much chance of surviving, at least not without some serious brain damage.

Mr Dreary was stood to his right and the other workmen were lurking around. One was quite tearful at the sight of his friend lying on the ground, while the others were sharing a cigarette between them, trying to console their nerves with smoking.

Victoria walked to the side of the fallen young man and knelt down. He was breathing shallowly. She felt for his pulse – no one stopped her – it was ragged and fluttery.

"Just came out of nowhere," Mr Dreary mumbled, his face ashen. "Just came out of nowhere."

"What precisely happened?" Victoria asked him.

Mr Dreary didn't seem to hear her. He certainly didn't answer. It was the teary-eyed workman who replied.

"Billy was taking some measurements of the brickwork here. We were trying to work out the best place to put the base for the scaffolding. We had just started clearing around this side so we could make a flat platform for the poles. The next thing we know, we hear a shout. One of the men, not sure who it was, said he saw something on top of the walls..."

Upon hearing this, Mr Dreary managed to snap out of his shocked delirium long enough to interrupt the workman.

"No one saw anybody on the walls!" He insisted. "What someone saw was a loose piece of masonry suddenly flying down. It came from up there."

He pointed his finger upwards towards the top of the tower. As far as Victoria could see, that particular piece of wall looked as solid as any of the rest. It didn't look as though it was in imminent danger of tumbling down. More to the point, she couldn't see a gap from which the large lump of stone had fallen.

Victoria swiftly surmised that she wasn't going to get a full answer from anybody while Mr Dreary was present. He wouldn't let them talk openly about what they saw.

"This piece of masonry fell down?" she asked, pointing out the slab that was lying beside Billy. "And hit him on the head?"

Comparing where the block of masonry sat and where the blood was on its edge, then looking at Billy's ruined head, she knew at once he had been moved.

"He must have fallen face first when he was hit, but someone has flipped him over?"

"That was me," the teary workman said. "I was trying to see if he was alive."

Victoria wasn't sure if that was a good thing, whether moving Billy might have made things worse, but by the looks of the injury and the unfortunate flatness of that particular area of Billy's skull, she doubted it had made much difference. It was a big piece of stone to have fallen onto his head. She was amazed he was still alive.

It was as that thought crossed her mind that she noticed Billy had become very still. She discreetly picked up his wrist and felt for the pulse. As she had feared, it was gone. Billy had become the second murder victim of their deadly tower phantom.

She decided it was best not to mention he was dead. She didn't think it would help the situation, and the doctor would be there soon enough to make the discovery. Such news usually came better from doctors.

Instead, she found herself looking at the piece of masonry. The first thing she noted was that there was a dark line around the base of the stone. It was on the opposite side to that which had fallen down on Billy. When she rubbed her finger across it, she realised the dark line was dampness on the stone. When she carefully moved around and looked at the base of the stone from another angle, she could see that it was still dirty from where it had once rested on the ground.

"This stone did not come from the top of the wall," she said aloud to the men around her. "This came from the rubble around the tower base. It had been sitting in the earth for who knows how long before someone pried it up. Look how dirty it is. It was sitting sunk about an inch in the ground before someone carried it all the way up to the top of the walls."

"Nonsense," Mr Dreary said at once, but there wasn't much heart in his denial.

"Why would anyone do that?" Lord Brooksby asked.

"I can think of a couple of reasons, but the first that springs to mind is that the masonry up on the battlements is not as loose as someone wants you to believe. It appears that our 'phantom' found it easier to bring a piece of already fallen stone up from the ground and drop it, than prising loose the stones of the battlements. When I say easier, it is relative, of course, but the evidence on that block of stone tells us all we need to know."

Lord Brooksby's gaze now wandered up to the tower and he took a deliberate step back wanting to be well out of the range of any further stones.

"There has to be a way up to the top of those walls for a person," Victoria remarked, looking upwards again herself. "There has to be a way to do it, and I don't think that whoever is perpetrating these crimes is climbing up the stonework. They couldn't have done that while carrying a stone. There has to be an easier way."

"No one can climb up there," Mr Dreary said firmly. "We've been around and around these walls."

"I saw that the stairs had fallen down long ago, at least those that led up from the tower floor," Victoria agreed with him. "There must be another way to get up there."

Victoria was starting to think about the cottage, how it abutted onto the walls of the tower. What if a doorway had been made, long ago, through to the tower to grant private access to the cottage occupants to the upper storeys of the ruins?

For that matter, what if the cottage had been built over an *existing* doorway, one that led into the internal hollow space between the walls where the old staircase had once run up the tower? If the tower had never meant to stand alone, and there had always been plans to build additions to it, perhaps additional doorways had been created that at the time seemed to lead to nowhere, but would ultimately be linked with another, future section of the castle?

But if there was a secret way into the tower from the cottage then Mr Woolmer had to know about it, yet he had said nothing. Did that mean he was working with whoever was behind these accidents for some unknown reason?

Victoria needed to get inside the cottage.

She moved towards Lord Brooksby and spoke softly, so they were not overheard.

"We should go back to the cottage," she told him, deciding it was better to instruct him rather than ask.

Lord Brooksby was in such a state of shock that telling him what to do was the only way to get him to do anything.

On the way back around the tower, they saw Mrs Nantwich lurking just inside the gates. Her courage had brought her that far, but no further.

"Mrs Nantwich, would you please come with us?" Victoria called out.

The basket weaver screwed up her face and looked as if she might refuse before she pursed her lips and nodded her determination to follow Victoria.

"There has to be a way from the cottage into the upper floor of the tower. It is the only solution that makes sense," Victoria explained to Brooksby and Mrs Nantwich. "If that is the case, then one has to wonder why Mr Woolmer has made no mention of this secret doorway."

Brooksby blustered at the suggestion his caretaker was in on the conspiracy, but they were almost at the cottage and a stern look from Victoria forced him into silence.

Mr Woolmer was stood in the doorway of his home looking agitated.

"How is the young fellow?" He asked his master.

"It is very serious, Mr Woolmer," Lord Brooksby said under Victoria's fierce gaze.

"I fear the doctor will find that the young man has sadly departed this life," Victoria added, wanting to see Woolmer's reaction to the news.

The person who reacted first, however, was Lord Brooksby.

"Good Lord! I didn't realise."

"I noticed he had stopped breathing and when I felt for his pulse there was nothing," Victoria elaborated. "I did not think it advisable to say this in front of the workmen."

Lord Brooksby looked fit to faint. Mr Woolmer rapidly darted inside the cottage and found him a chair. Once he had positioned it just within the doorway, he took his employer's arm and ushered him into it. Brooksby was roughing his hair up, dishevelling the neatly parted hairstyle that he had oiled down that morning and turning it into a ragged mess.

"Well, this is surely the end of everything. I barely got them to return to work after the last accident. It took considerable money to persuade Mr Dreary to convince his men it was bad luck and not some curse upon the tower. He promised he would get his men to stay silent about the things they had seen around the site, and that no one would mention any spectre or someone lurking about the top of the ruins. I won't be able to bribe him this time, will I?"

"I doubt it," Victoria replied. "Truthfully, I'm not sure it's fair to ask Dreary and his men to keep working here until we have resolved this mystery. It is quite obvious the perpetrator is willing to hurt them. To kill them. We can't have them placed in any further danger."

"If I had thought there was such a danger to them, I never would have asked them to continue," Lord Brooksby said hastily, feeling guilt that he was responsible for Billy's death by insisting the men keep working.

"What is done is done," Victoria consoled him. "We now have to move forward and resolve this matter. I need to speak to you, Mr Woolmer."

Woolmer had started to look uneasy. His face had fallen and if ever a man looked guilty, it was the unhappy caretaker.

"You wish to speak to me, miss?" He said, his earlier belligerence vanished.

"I believe there is a secret way from this cottage into the tower," Victoria told him. "I am going upstairs to find this doorway and demonstrate how someone is climbing to the top of the tower and throwing stones at people. Do you understand?"

Mr Woolmer's lips moved as if he was going to protest, but he said nothing.

"Very good," Victoria responded; perhaps the man had at last realised the seriousness of the situation.

Victoria moved to the staircase that she could see running up the back wall. Mrs Nantwich followed her, after all these years she wanted to know what was upstairs in those rooms. The staircase dog-legged and turned back on itself, before they reached a narrow landing at the front of the cottage, with a doorway on either side of them. Victoria glanced through the door on the right, seeing that it led into a bedroom. There was a large double bed just visible from where she stood. They headed into the bedroom to take a quick look around. There was nothing remarkable, it was kept tidy, and the bed was freshly made-up.

"Well, that is as we expected," Mrs Nantwich said.

They walked across to the room on the opposite side of the landing. Victoria tried the door and immediately discovered that it was locked.

"He didn't say anything about a key," Victoria was annoyed,

but not entirely surprised that Mr Woolmer had neglected this information.

They headed back downstairs to retrieve the key. They had left Mr Woolmer with Lord Brooksby in the kitchen. When they entered the room they found his lordship alone, leaning across the table with his head down on his arms.

"Do you feel unwell, your Lordship?" Mrs Nantwich rushed to him and placed a hand on his shoulder.

"Just a little shaken up," Brooksby replied. "I have a sudden headache, I fear from all this anxiety."

Victoria was glancing around the kitchen. She had instantly noted the absence of Mr Woolmer.

"Where is your caretaker?"

"Mr Woolmer went to the front room to fetch me something stronger than tea," Brooksby replied. "He said he had some whisky in there."

Victoria walked back into the hallway and across into the comfortable sitting room. Not to her surprise, there was no sign of Mr Woolmer or his whisky. He had bolted. Which only confirmed to her that he knew about the secret of the tower and felt it advisable to run away.

Might Mr Woolmer have been behind this all along?

He was a spry old man, and he would have had plenty of time to learn the cottage's secrets. If that was the case, why had he done it? He had a comfortable job as the caretaker of the castle, one he would happily have for life. It didn't seem logical for him to start throwing stones at people and risk all that.

Victoria walked out of the house and looked around her, trying to catch a glimpse of the caretaker, but he had a head start and had disappeared. There was no way of knowing where he had gone.

Mrs Nantwich appeared at the front door.

"What is the matter?"

"Mr Woolmer has run away," Victoria told her bluntly. "Seems to me he knows a lot more about the secrets of that upstairs room than he wanted to let on."

Mrs Nantwich did not know how to reply. She was thinking about all the times she had offered to sweep those upstairs rooms, never suspecting there was a locked door and a secret route into the tower.

"Mrs Ward knew about this secret too."

Victoria nodded at her.

"Mrs Ward must have known the cottage's secrets. The real question is, what were they both hiding? What was so important that they were prepared to kill someone over it?"

Mrs Nantwich did not know what to say. Victoria realised she was out of her depth. She really needed to speak to her uncle and reveal this new information so they could formulate a plan. Just as she was thinking all this, the doctor finally arrived. He started to move towards her, clearly thinking the patient he had been summoned to see was inside the cottage.

"Mrs Nantwich, could you please look after Lord Brooksby and make sure he is recovered enough to go home. I shall see to everything else," Victoria spoke quickly.

Mrs Nantwich nodded her agreement as Victoria headed off to intercept the doctor. "This way doctor, your patient is just around here, though I fear you are too late."

The doctor, with his bushy whiskers and top hat, frowned at her.

"Not the first time I've been too late to help someone who has had an accident here," he said. "Truly, this place must be cursed."

Twelve

Bainbridge had concluded his reading for the day and had made an assortment of notes on some paper Mr Savage had kindly provided for him. He was just beginning to think about his dinner when a knock came on his door. It was followed almost immediately by Victoria darting in before he had a chance to say she could enter. That was Victoria all over; when something was on her mind and she was agitated, she very rarely took heed of doors being shut.

The first thing Bainbridge noticed was the frazzled look on her face; the lines around her mouth spoke volumes and filled him with a mounting sense of apprehension. The second thing he noticed were the speckles of blood on her dress. In her haste to examine the fallen workman, Victoria had accidentally trailed a sleeve over his head wound and picked up some of his blood.

"What has happened?" Bainbridge said, rising immediately.

Victoria raised a hand and motioned that he should sit down again.

"I am sorry to say that another workman has been attacked by the phantom, and in this instance, he has been killed."

Victoria described her whole day to Bainbridge, from her interview with Mr Dreary to her conversation with Mrs Nantwich about the mysterious and secretive Mrs Ward, finishing with the death of Billy at the tower and Mr Woolmer's disappearance.

"We searched all over the house after the doctor had seen to Billy, but neither me nor Mrs Nantwich could find a key for that upper room," Victoria explained. "We will have to get a locksmith out unless we want to break the door down."

"It sounds as though you have done some thorough investigating today," Bainbridge nodded. "What has happened is truly appalling. That poor young man."

"It is just criminal. So cruel and unnecessary."

Victoria took a seat opposite her uncle. She sat down heavily, wariness dragging down her limbs. There was nothing like seeing a young, innocent man murdered to take the soul out of you.

"All this violence and death for the sake of some secret we have yet to reveal," Bainbridge muttered to himself.

"We have to get into that secret room in the cottage, find out if I'm correct, and that there is a passage leading from it up to the top of the tower. Maybe we will even find some clue as to who is behind this. Though I am beginning to suspect Mr Woolmer."

"He is spry enough to do the job," Bainbridge nodded. "But I cannot see his motivation. More likely, he stumbled across the same secret Mrs Ward was familiar with and has been bribed or threatened into silence. How curious. By the way, a gentleman called Mr Hollobone loaned me the late Mrs Ward's novel, the one she wrote while she was in the cottage next to the tower. It's not particularly exciting. A rather mundane gothic romance, the usual sort of thing. Two girls and a young man, one believes she loves him, he loves the other, the first then discovers that her love is unrequited, and it all becomes messy."

"Does it have anything in it about secret passages?"

"No," Bainbridge said. "In fact, I think the book is something of a red herring. There's nothing in it to suggest what might have been going on at the tower. But I did have a very interesting conversation with Mr Hollobone about how the tower appears to be missing its dungeon. Hollobone and other historians believe that the place should have a space beneath it, somewhere Baron Fitzhubert could keep his enemies. That the tower is missing such a place has always troubled people, apparently."

"So now we have a secret dungeon to find as well?"

"Could be nothing," Bainbridge answered. "On the other hand, it could be something. What was his lordship's thoughts after the accident?"

"Lord Brooksby is calling off work on the site," Victoria explained. "He sent all the workmen home."

"I would like to speak to the workmen and see if they can give us any more information about the figure that has been seen around the site. How disappointing that Brooksby did not appreciate the seriousness of the situation earlier. If he had done so, then maybe that young man would not be dead."

"We were all inclined to tell him to keep going," Victoria pointed out. "We all thought that he shouldn't give in to the saboteur."

"We were utterly wrong," Bainbridge became sorrowful. "I am very disheartened by this news. But the first thing we need to do is keep investigating. We will catch this killer; of that I am determined."

"We will need to send for a locksmith to open that upper room," Victoria added. "Maybe there will be some clue in there as to our saboteur?"

"A shame Mrs Ward is no longer with us to tell us about her own experiences in the cottage," Bainbridge mulled. "I wonder who we could speak to concerning her? Who sold the Brooksbys the cottage and the castle in the first place? My understanding is she didn't have any children, so it must have been another relative."

"Presumably one who knew nothing about the strange secrets there," Victoria remarked.

"Or simply wanted the place off his hands and cared nothing for its secrets. That is another line of investigation we should perhaps follow up at some point."

"I'm glad to see you are feeling a great deal better," Victoria smiled at her uncle, noting that he did look back to his usual self.

There was a healthy colour to his face, and he was no longer sniffling and sneezing.

"Colds very rarely trouble me for long. It was merely a passing affliction, and I feel quite myself again. Besides, there is a case that needs to be investigated. No cold will deter me from that."

"Lord Brooksby has given me permission to do anything I want at the cottage. He gave me the key to it. We don't know if there's another key, of course. Probably there is. But for now, at least, we can lock the place up."

"What did the doctor make of the young Billy's accident?"

"Same as before. He was satisfied that something had fallen from the top of the tower, and it was pure bad luck it had hit Billy on the head. I did briefly raise the suggestion that a police constable should be informed, but he just shook his head. Lord Brooksby also doesn't want this going any further."

"No, I believe we shall be on our own with this mystery. The police will not take an interest until we can prove that there is a real person behind these 'accidents.' Who is this Mrs Nantwich, you've become friendly with?"

"A very sensible older lady in the local area who has walked past the tower all her life and only recently noticed a figure lurking around. She is of the same opinion that it was the building of the fence that triggered everything."

"I think she is right. Someone is trying to hide something," Bainbridge nodded his head. "Whatever their secret is, it must have been going on for many years, even to the days of Mrs Ward. For some reason, she agreed to keep this secret during her lifetime, only after her death did a problem arise and someone became afraid their secret would come out."

"What sort of secret do you think we are talking about?"

"It could be many things. It could be someone trying to hide that they're a criminal on the run. Perhaps there is a body hidden somewhere around those ruins, maybe more than one body, and the person responsible for them being there is trying to hide up their crime," Bainbridge was thoughtful a moment. "The innkeeper will certainly know of a good locksmith, and I would rather tackle that task tonight then leave it until the morning. Has Lord Brooksby gone home?"

"Yes, I felt it was for the best. He was not in a state to be useful."

"Poor man has certainly had his fair share of bad news lately. An innocent victim in all this, I fear. Terrible, really. Whoever is behind all this, they are cold blooded and cold hearted. They don't care who they hurt, just so long as they're not interfered with."

"Then we ought to be very, very careful," Victoria responded. "Because once we start poking our noses deeper into this matter, we are going to become the prime targets for this killer."

"That is very much what I am hoping for," Bainbridge grinned at her. "Let them make a move against us, that will assist us enormously."

Victoria was not so enthusiastic about becoming a target for a murderer. But she knew exactly what her uncle meant. They had to lure out this killer somehow, and if that meant using themselves as bait, then so be it.

Thirteen

Mr Savage was able to provide them with the name of a reliable locksmith. Within the next hour, the gentleman was at Mr Woolmer's Cottage, where he found Bainbridge and Victoria waiting for him.

It was now dusky, and a mist was floating across the ground. The tower looked even spookier in the damp moonlight. When Lord Brooksby had left, he had not bothered to shut the gates behind him. They now stood open. However, there was no sign that anybody from the town wished to wander in. Maybe even the townsfolk had become anxious about the supposed phantom at the tower and had opted not to go near the ruins.

Aside from the cries of a night owl and the rustling in the bushes as the wind whipped around, there was no sign of anybody. Mr Savage, however, had promised them that the locksmith he recommended would not be put off by the circumstances of his visit, nor cowed by the sight of the haunted tower.

The gentleman went by the name of Horner. He was a slender fellow of indeterminate years. The sort of person who might only be forty or yet might be sixty. He had a loping gait and seemed to lift his knees a little higher than necessary when he walked. He promised them he was extremely dexterous with locks and showed off his elegant long fingers.

"No lock in this world can defy me," he said proudly.

"And you are not concerned to go near the tower?" Bainbridge had to ask, just to reassure himself.

Mr Horner shrugged.

"Just another little challenge to add to the mix," he said with a grin.

Not that Bainbridge thought anything else would occur that night. The drama of the unfortunate death of Billy surely had satisfied the ghoul who was ambushing people around the tower for the time being. The disappearance of Mr Woolmer might even have convinced the 'phantom' to slip away as well.

They reached the cottage and Bainbridge unlocked the door. The cold, misty night air had brought back Bainbridge's cold with a vengeance, and he was sniffling into a handkerchief as they went up the cottage's narrow staircase.

"It must be over a decade since I was last in this cottage," Mr Horner told them in conversation. "That lady writer invited me here. She had a cupboard with a stout lock on it and she'd lost the key. Needed me to undo it so she could get out her typewriter."

"What was she like?" Victoria asked him.

They now stood in front of the locked door.

"What was she like?" Mr Horner repeated the question to himself as he mused on it. "She seemed pleasant enough. A bit up herself, but aren't they all those ones who write? She wore glasses, I remember that. Someone told me that if you did a job for her, she would give you a book of poems and I thought, well, that would be dandy because my wife loves poems. But she didn't give me anything except the money for the job, so I suppose that wasn't true. Or maybe she didn't have any books of poems lying about."

Victoria didn't think she was going to get much more from the gentleman, but she asked anyway.

"Did she seem the sort of person to keep secrets. Did she ever do anything when you were here to suggest she was hiding something?"

Mr Horner gave her a frown of confusion at this statement, then almost laughed.

"Well, that's not what I was expecting you to ask. I don't think she did. I can't say I was paying too much attention. I did wonder that she would lock her typewriter up in a cabinet, but then I suppose she always went home at night, and she perhaps fancied that someone might break in and steal it. She was precious about that typewriter."

"I have talked to someone else who informed me that Ethel never stayed here overnight, despite the fact that there was a perfectly serviceable bedroom upstairs."

Mr Horner had clearly not concerned himself about this, or ever given it any thought.

"Some people like their own beds," he answered philosophically.

Bainbridge was still perched on the landing just beneath them, sniffling into his handkerchief.

"Might we get on with opening that lock now? I'm starting to want to go back to my bed."

Victoria glanced to her uncle while Mr Horner got to work on the lock. He was looking a little pale and there was redness around his eyes.

"Maybe you ought to go back to the inn?" she suggested, stepping down a stair or two and touching his shoulder. "I can look after this matter."

"No, I want to see this thing through to the end, and my curiosity outweighs my fever. Still, let's not hang around, shall we?"

Mr Horner had produced various tools out of a small pouch that he carried on his belt. He was carefully inserting them in the lock. For a time he didn't say anything as he concentrated on his job, but it was only a matter of moments before the lock clicked and released.

"Wasn't much of a bother," he told them with a smile. "Quite an old-style lock, easy to undo for me."

He finished by opening the door for them and holding it wide while first Victoria and then Bainbridge headed into the room.

What they found behind the door was very much what they had expected. It was a second bedroom. The bed was still ruffled up, as if someone had been sleeping in it recently. There were tatty curtains at the window and a chair to one side bearing a man's flat cap. There was an aura about the room, as if someone had just left in haste.

The space was not large, and one of the walls had a slightly concave shape to it due to it being abutted against the wall of the castle. Efforts had been made to turn this wall into a flat surface, but you could still see how the plaster slightly curved. Bainbridge went over to this far wall and tapped at the floor with his walking stick. There was a giant wardrobe against it, nearly taking up the entire space. The sort of wardrobe that one would not expect for such a small room as it seemed to overwhelm the place. That gave Bainbridge an idea.

He now attempted to peer behind the wardrobe.

There was no light in the room other than a rather small lantern they had brought up from the kitchen, and the shadows behind the wardrobe limited his view.

"Vicky, shine some light over here for me, will you?"

Victoria headed over to her uncle and held up the lantern to cast a light just behind the wardrobe. Bainbridge smiled.

"I think there is a hollow space behind this wardrobe."

Victoria looked at the monstrous piece of furniture.

"Do you want us to move it? The item looks particularly heavy. It will take two of us and how are we going to squeeze it out around the bed to make enough room to go behind it? There isn't enough room either side to simply slide it across."

"No, no, our phantom would be far more practical than to have to move this every time he wished to depart through the wall," Bainbridge said firmly. "Let's open the doors of this wardrobe. There must be a way through it."

Victoria went to open the doors, but they resisted her. They were locked as well. Fortunately, Mr Horner was still present, and as he heard the doors resisting her, he beamed brightly and came over with his tools. Nothing made him happier than unlocking reluctant doors. He made short work of the wardrobe lock and opened the doors wide.

What they saw within was a dark, shadowy space. Victoria held up the lamp. There was a jacket hanging in the wardrobe to one side, but at first glance there seemed to be no entranceway. Then she noticed something within the shadows cast by the dim glow of the lantern; it almost looked like the back of the wardrobe was filled with a solid, black void. When she reached in with her hand, she realised the 'void' was an illusion created by fabric.

Stepping one foot into the wardrobe, she reached for a corner and found the fabric was pinned in place. She removed the pins carefully and peeled back the material, slowly revealing what was behind it.

"My word," Horner said, staring as the old forgotten doorway into the tower revealed itself.

"This is how the phantom gets to the top of the tower," Victoria said to her uncle.

Bainbridge was smiling brightly, pleased that they had found a solution to part of the mystery. Victoria took the lantern from him and now stepped carefully into the dark space beyond the wardrobe. She held the lantern low so she could see the floor. The doorway was cut through the stone of the tower and was solid beneath her feet. She came out into a passageway sandwiched between the outer and inner wall of the tower. To her left, there was a staircase winding up as far as she could see; if it were complete it would take her to the top of the tower.

"Do be careful Vicky, I don't feel in quite the fit condition to follow you," Bainbridge called out from behind.

Victoria glanced back for a moment, a slight apprehension coming over her. Going up those stairs in the dark, not knowing who could be at the top, was slightly daunting. She was not afraid of ghosts, but she *was* afraid of people masquerading as ghosts, especially when they liked to kill people.

"I will follow you if you like, miss," Horner volunteered, he looked quite keen to climb up the stairs himself and see the town from the top of the tower.

Victoria would be glad of his company. She nodded her head to him, and he stepped through the wardrobe onto the stone stairs behind her. Together, they began to carefully mount the steps.

As Victoria had anticipated, this staircase had survived better than the one below. It reached all the way up to the battlements of the tower, winding around the second floor and emerging where there would once have been a wooden roof. Up here, she had a magnificent view of the landscape around her, though staring out into the blackness of the night made her feel somewhat giddy. The ground far below seemed to disappear as if there was nothing there.

The mist that had been forming earlier was now swirling into a dense fog making it difficult to see much in the lantern light. Victoria, however, noticed that there were cigarette ends scattered on the walkway, as if someone had spent a great deal of time up here, smoking while they waited for someone to stand in just the right place. She pictured the phantom slipping up here secretly to wait for just the right opportunity to make another 'accident' happen.

She leaned over the edge of the tower and got a dose of vertigo as she did so. She quickly stepped back. Horner seeing her move fast, grasped at her elbow.

"Did you feel faint, miss?"

"Just for a moment," Victoria shook him off. "When you look over the side it's so dark, it's like staring into a pit."

Horner was intrigued enough to look for himself. He leaned over the stonework battlement and peered down.

"Cor, you are right! Like looking down into a bottomless barrel."

Victoria decided she had had enough of the battlements. The fog was cold and damp and starting to leach through her shawl – she had been cold and damp enough the previous night and didn't want to suffer it again. She suggested to Horner that they set off back down the stairs and he said he would go ahead just to make sure she didn't fall. As gentlemanly and chivalrous as this act was, Victoria was pained by the fact that he obviously thought she was a fragile woman liable to suddenly faint. It had just been a passing moment of dizziness that anyone could have suffered from.

Bainbridge was waiting for them in the bedroom, sitting on the dishevelled bed.

"Well?" He asked, coughing into his handkerchief.

"It is exactly as we expected. A staircase leads all the way up to the battlements. You don't need to be a phantom or a monkey to get up there."

"This raises considerably more questions. Was Mr Woolmer the person who was sneaking up to the battlements? Or is there an accomplice, someone who Mrs Ward also knew about all those years ago?"

"How curious," Horner said, getting excited about the whole

situation. "You are saying that there was someone using this secret passage when Mrs Ward had the house?"

"It is only a supposition," Bainbridge told him quickly. "Based on a few things we have been told about the woman. It could be complete nonsense. The phantom may have only appeared after the Brooksbys took over this land and decided to make it private. The question remains though, why is this person intent on hurting the Brooksbys and anyone associated with them?"

"There were remains of cigarettes on the battlements. By the looks of it, someone has spent a lot of time up there watching what's been going on," Victoria added. "Could they have a personal vendetta against the Brooksby family?"

"I think it more likely they are trying to protect a secret that has lain undisturbed here for years."

"If there is a secret or secrets here, they must be exceptionally well hidden," Victoria shook her head. "I've walked all around the base of the tower and found nothing."

"But that is exactly how you hide secrets. You make sure they look very ordinary and boring," Bainbridge was tapping at his chin. "I would like to explore the connection this mystery has to Mrs Ward. Perhaps tomorrow we ought to find out more about her and her family."

Mr Horner was listening to all this. He had had a very interesting evening and was deeply glad he had agreed to respond to this particular call for help. His wife had told him it was too late and too dark to go on such an escapade, and surely the lock could wait until the morning. But he had wanted to be useful, and Mr Savage had suggested that his help was needed urgently.

What a story he had to tell his wife and the fellows in the pub later on!

Bainbridge started to cough again. He looked tired, his shoulders slumping. Victoria wanted him back in his bed, tucked up in the warm. She went over to him and tugged at his elbow.

"I should never have allowed you to come out,"

"Since when do you get to tell me what I do and don't do?" Bainbridge scolded her.

Victoria just shook her head.

"I should have *advised* you not to come out," she corrected.

Bainbridge levered himself up to his feet. He was feeling achy all over, his head was pounding and when he moved his feet the floor felt alarmingly spongey, as if it were not beneath his feet at all. Not to mention his streaming nose and sore throat. He made no more conversation as they all headed back downstairs.

"Where is Mr Woolmer?" Horner asked as they reached the ground floor.

He was not aware that the caretaker had departed in haste.

"I hope no accident has befallen him. I heard what happened to Billy earlier today."

Horner pulled a face, grimacing as he thought about the maliciousness of whoever had been lurking at the top of the tower and pretending to be a phantom. "I would like to say a bad word about that person and what they did to poor Billy. His mother is devastated."

"Mr Woolmer has departed," Victoria said carefully, thinking it was probably best not to mention Mr Woolmer had run away and looked likely to be involved in the phantom situation.

There was no knowing what might happen if people in the local town realised the caretaker could be behind the demise of young Billy. The last thing they needed was people taking justice into their own hands.

Mr Horner didn't ask anything further about Mr Woolmer. They left the cottage and locked the door behind them, then moved towards the gates. Horner said his farewells and headed along the road to their left, while they turned to the right to return to the inn. Victoria had her arm through her uncle's.

"I don't know if what we have discovered will make things better for Lord Brooksby or worse. But at least we're now closer to determining who is responsible for the death of his father," Victoria said.

Bainbridge coughed politely into his handkerchief.

"It might not provide him any consolation. But we should be able to bring him some justice. The treachery of Mr Woolmer will certainly bite at him hard."

Victoria nodded her head.

"Just what is going on here?" She wondered.

Fourteen

Bainbridge looked very sorry for himself when they returned to the inn. Victoria ensured he was tucked up in bed and Mr Savage asked his wife to make him a hot cup of tea with a slug of whisky and some honey stirred in. He promised this was the perfect remedy for a cold and Bainbridge would feel right as rain in the morning.

Victoria was not so optimistic and anticipated that her uncle would still be in bed the next day when she rose. She was not surprised, therefore, to find him exactly where she had left him when she tapped on his door the next morning.

Bainbridge's cold had blossomed into full-blown influenza. He made no attempt to rise from the bed and looked at her through puffy, red eyes.

"I am of no use to you today, Victoria," he told her sadly. "I shall have to remain here and recuperate."

"I advise you don't move out of that bed at all," Victoria responded. "But of course you can choose to ignore that."

This managed to bring a smile to Bainbridge's lips; after their conversation of the night before, his niece had remembered that she couldn't *tell* him what to do, but she was allowed to *advise* him.

"I am going to attempt to make contact with Mrs Ward's family,"

Victoria explained to him. "I want to see if they can tell me a bit more about her time at the cottage. I'm sure Lord Brooksby will be able to give me her relatives' names."

"Be careful Victoria, we're getting close to a very deep secret. One which I suspect has been kept hidden for a long time and which people are desperate not to reveal."

Victoria nodded her head.

"I shall be discreet and, since I would appreciate an introduction from Lord Brooksby to help my enquiries run smoothly, I intend to ask him to accompany me."

They chatted for a few moments more, Victoria making an in-depth enquiry into Bainbridge's health which rapidly tried his patience. Only after he made further promises that he wasn't going to move from his bed that day was Victoria satisfied and departed to make her way back to the tower.

It was a grey day, but it was dry. She wondered if they would get some sunshine later, or whether it would once again begin to rain. No matter if it did, she had her umbrella with her today, and her walking boots were just about dried out from her previous escapades.

When she reached the tower, the gates were still stood open, and the place looked sadly abandoned. The workmen had not returned to work that morning. After the drama of the day before, she was not sure if Lord Brooksby would turn up either, though they had an arrangement he would meet them at the tower every morning to discuss the case. If he did not arrive in his carriage, then she would have to go back and get the car and drive to his estate, which would be an inconvenient waste of time, especially as she was not entirely sure where his house was. Victoria was never fond of driving places without a navigator, especially in the countryside. Maps of the countryside, in her experience, were typically inadequate and very rarely got you to where you wanted to be.

To while away the time until Lord Brooksby (hopefully) arrived. Victoria walked up to the cottage and tried the door to see that it was still locked.

It was.

She had the key with her, so she let herself inside. She took a walk around the kitchen first, looking for any signs of this second person that she assumed had been here with Mr Woolmer. Her assumption that a second individual was involved in the crime was based on the logical argument that Woolmer seemed unlikely to have come up with this scheme of throwing masonry at his former employer. What would be the point? Far more logical that someone else had interfered. Someone who had a hold over Mr Woolmer and could therefore convince him to do what he wanted and keep quiet about it.

There was no sign, however, at least downstairs of this second man. In the sitting room that Mrs Ward had once used as her writing study Victoria noticed a pretty rosewood table that still bore marks on its surface to show where a typewriter had routinely graced it. She went to the only cupboard in the room, again an elegant rosewood item, and opened the doors to reveal a typewriter within. Clearly, the family had not considered it necessary to remove the item after Mrs Ward's death. In fact, by the state of the cottage, it seemed they had left the entire place as it had been when she died. Victoria wondered if that might assist her. Might the deceased writer have left a clue behind?

She took the typewriter out of the cupboard and glanced over it for a moment. She could see it had been well used. Some of the letters on the keys were worn almost completely away. On another shelf in the cupboard was fresh paper, several sheafs of notes and early drafts of the manuscript for her novel about the tower. Victoria pulled one of these out and thumbed through it idly. Bainbridge had already read the entire novel that Mrs Ward had written and did not believe it contained any clues as to what might be going on at the tower.

Victoria pulled out some more papers and found a bundle that contained historical notes about Bungay and the castle itself. Most of the details she had already learned; the story of Baron Fitzhubert and his nefarious dealings which had led to his execution seemed to be the main piece of history that anybody in the town was interested in. Other legends listed in the notes included the black dog that had slipped through the church wreaking destruction, and a phantom monkey said to sometimes be seen in the town square.

As Victoria read through the stories, she recognised them from the volume on ghost legends that Bainbridge had mentioned to her. Victoria surmised that Mrs Ward had read the same book and made notes about some of the stories perhaps for her own work.

She was about to return the papers to where she had found them, when she caught a glimpse of the title of the last story on the back page.

The supposed treasure of Bungay.

Her curiosity was piqued; she had just started to read the page, when she heard the clatter of carriage wheels outside and realised that Lord Brooksby had turned up at last. She deposited the papers on the table and hurried out of the cottage.

Lord Brooksby nervously walked through the gates onto his land. He looked up at the castle ruins and then to Victoria.

"I wasn't sure you would be here," he said.

"Well, I have a case to solve," Victoria responded. "My uncle is still indisposed by his cold, but there is something I must show you."

She waved to Lord Brooksby and escorted him into the house and upstairs to the back bedroom that abutted the castle walls. There she opened up the wardrobe for him and showed him the hidden doorway. Brooksby's long face became even longer as his jaw dropped.

"Is that...?"

"You are looking at the way the phantom has been accessing the tower. This staircase winds all the way up to the battlements. Come on, I'll show you."

Victoria encouraged Lord Brooksby to follow her up the staircase. His lordship hesitated as they reached the battlements, feeling overcome by the distance he now found himself standing above the ground. He stood and stared around him.

"You can see for miles," he said in a whisper, as if speaking louder would somehow break the spell that had come over him. "Right across the town."

Lord Brooksby turned around in a small circle, agog at the view he saw.

"Then Woolmer knew about this? Wait, is he the phantom?"

"If he is, it seems a curious thing for him to do. Why would he attack your family? Why would he become so protective of this tower? After all, you had given him a comfortable place to retire with a cottage all of his own."

"I always thought that Woolmer was loyal to the family and close to my father. He had been in our employ for all of his life. We gave him this place as the caretaker, thinking it was a good place for him to spend his final years, while still performing a service for the family. Woolmer would have despised charity, so we found him a role that was easy enough but made him feel useful."

"Does Mr Woolmer smoke cigarettes?" Victoria picked up one of the discarded cigarettes from the floor of the battlements and showed it to Lord Brooksby.

"No, he always smokes a pipe."

Victoria nodded her head.

"I am confident there is a second person involved in this case," she continued. "I don't know why they're here. I don't know how they came to associate with Woolmer, but I think until we know the full story, we have to assume that he has been forced to assist them one way or the other."

Brooksby didn't know what to think. He was still shaken up by the hidden passage Victoria had discovered. He now had proof his father had been murdered, but he was not sure if that made things any better.

"Could you perhaps take me to the home of Mrs Ward's family today?" Victoria asked him. "I would appreciate it if you could make an introduction for me to them. I would like to know more about the lady who owned this cottage before you did."

"I can do that," Brooksby agreed. "But why would you wish to speak to her family?"

"I think Mrs Ward knew about this secret way up to the tower, and I think she was keeping other secrets too. But what those secrets were, I'm not sure. I think it would be useful to speak to her family to discover if there is a connection between this ghost saga and someone who was known to her. If the events occurring now overlap with events that happened to Mrs Ward, that may reveal to us motive for this mystery."

"If you say so," Brooksby agreed. "Do you wish to travel there now?"

Victoria did; she liked to strike while the iron was hot. They headed back downstairs, locked up the cottage, and returned to Lord Brooksby's carriage. He instructed his coachman where to go next, and they headed out of the town.

"I take it you never met Mrs Ethel Ward?" Victoria asked his lordship as they rode.

"No, I never had the pleasure. I have read her novel. My father gathered any books or documents he could find concerning the tower and that was one of them. Mrs Ward owned the cottage and the abutting tower for around 20 years. She used the cottage as her private writing place, gaining inspiration, it is said, from the ruins next to her. Her great masterpiece was, of course, her novel about Bungay castle."

Victoria thought about this alleged masterpiece, which Bainbridge had considered mediocre at best. But who was she to judge?

"Did she have family? Children?"

"No, Mrs Ward had no immediate family, and she outlived her husband by some years. Upon her death the whole estate went to a cousin. This cousin then went about selling off various portions of the estate to cover Mrs Ward's outstanding debts and the death duties. There was a house somewhere out in the countryside, and that went first, followed by the cottage and the ruins. My father was very excited to get hold of those."

"Mrs Ward's cousin lives in this county?" Victoria asked.

"Fortunately, he does. Otherwise we would not be able to visit him so swiftly. He is an older, retired gentleman who mainly spends his time in his garden. I remember meeting him at the time we completed the sale for the castle ruins. We drank tea together and ate cake while my father finished signing the documents."

Victoria was beginning to think that this cousin might not be terribly helpful in revealing to her Mrs Ward's secrets. It was possible he didn't know anything about his cousin's life in Bungay. Victoria feared that whatever secrets Mrs Ward knew had died with her.

The carriage clattered down a series of country roads, some little more than lanes. The coachman never broke the horses' pace and didn't seem concerned when they bumped over potholes or found themselves running between two tight hedgerows that scraped the sides of the carriage. Lord Brooksby didn't seem troubled either, but then he was used to this sort of travel. He was, after all, a country squire.

They eventually came to a house with tall stone walls and massive gates. Ivy was crawling over the walls and the gates stood open. The coachman swung in through them tightly and there was a moment, as Victoria rocked to one side, that she fancied a wheel might have actually lifted up off the ground. Then they were clattering along an old driveway between lime trees.

Victoria popped her head out of the window so that she could see the house they were approaching. It was a grand Georgian pile with a grey roof and tall windows.

"What is the name of Mrs Ward's cousin?" She asked Lord Brooksby.

"Mr Crookshaw," Brooksby replied immediately. "Of the Norfolk Crookshaws. A man who has extensive influence within the area."

The carriage rattled to a halt in front of a massive, pillared portico. A butler had already appeared on the doorstep to see who the visitors were. The coachman dropped down from his seat and opened the door for Lord Brooksby. Lord Brooksby in turn held out his hand to Victoria and helped her down. Victoria was more inclined to jump down by herself but decided it would be more prudent to hold back and act like a lady for once. Sometimes it was better to remember your manners when you were dealing with the upper classes, just in case they took against you simply because you did not behave like a smart young lady.

She also was acutely aware she was still wearing her walking boots and desperately hoped no one would notice them.

Brooksby escorted her up the steps beneath the portico and spoke politely to the butler, explaining that they hoped to see his master if he was in.

The butler showed no indication of either interest or consternation about their appearance and departed into the house. He returned a short time later and informed them that his master would gladly see them and that he was currently in the library. They were shown through into an extensive hall with a staircase that swooped up at the back and led off into various rooms. The walls were lined with tall paintings. Victoria spied a rather nice portrait of a young couple in regency clothes. The lady smiled softly at the viewer, while the gentleman was dashingly handsome. She wondered if these were ancestors of Mr Crookshaw.

The butler took them up the staircase, down a short corridor and into a library. His master proved to be an elderly gentleman seated in a Bath chair. He smiled at them brightly. He was wearing a smoking jacket and appeared to be still in his pyjamas. He had a face that had sagged gracefully with age and merged into its lines, creating a cheerful and welcoming countenance. He pushed himself back gently from the table, the wheels of the Bath chair squeaking.

"What an unexpected pleasure, Lord Brooksby, to see you again."

"I am sorry about the intrusion so early in the morning," Brooksby responded. "May I introduce Miss Victoria Bovington? She wished to meet you as she wanted to know a little bit more about your cousin Ethel Ward."

"Does she now?" Mr Crookshaw was intrigued. "And what is your interest in my cousin, dear lady?"

"I have read her novel," Victoria swiftly adapted the truth to suit her purpose. "And I've been in her cottage, courtesy of Lord Brooksby. I handled her typewriter only just today. I would love to know a little bit more about the woman behind the writing."

"A fanatic of my dear cousin's work, I see! Well, Ethel would surely be delighted to have spoken to you if she were still alive. She loved to speak to those who enjoyed her writing. As she is deceased, I shall do my best to accommodate you. Please won't you come take a seat?"

There were two leather sofas either side of a fireplace in the library. Mr Crookshaw motioned to them, and then managed to wheel himself over in his Bath chair. Victoria briefly wondered if she ought to offer to assist him, but she feared she might infringe on his sense of pride. Mr Crookshaw appeared to be quite capable of taking himself back and forth to the fireplace in his chair.

"Where would you like me to begin, young lady? I can tell you so much about my cousin. We grew up together, though sadly we grew apart in our adult years."

"I want to know about her time at the cottage. I'm told she was inspired by being there to write her novel."

Mr Crookshaw nodded his head.

"The cottage was her space to write. I remember she came to visit me one day, it must have been around my birthday, and she told me how she had been to Bungay and saw a notice that the cottage was up for sale. She made inquiries at once. She had wanted to have a connection to that castle for so long. Even as a child she was fascinated by the ruins and all the stories that accompanied them. When she heard the price of the cottage, she simply couldn't resist, and her husband agreed to buy it there and then.

"Neither of them was ever very good with money, and they were in a great deal of debt when she passed away, which is why I had to sell the cottage almost at once. I would much rather have hung on to it for a little longer. I didn't even have time to make arrangements to remove all her furniture. Instead, I sold it as it was to Lord Brooksby."

"I notice that Mrs Ward seemed to be very interested in the history of Bungay," Victoria added. "When I was looking at her typewriter, I came across her notes about the legends and stories of the town. She seemed fascinated by the local folklore."

"Oh yes, the folklore was the thing that caught her attention," Mr Crookshaw nodded. "She could spend hours telling you about demon dogs and their place in Bungay's history. Not to mention all the stuff about Baron Fitzhubert. She told me once that she was quite hopeful she would see his ghost one day."

"It struck me she was also interested in the secrets that a place like the tower could hold," Victoria hoped to prise something useful out of Mr Crookshaw.

The old gentleman tipped his head on one side and looked at her curiously.

"Secrets," he said, a smile on his lips. "Oh, my cousin did like secrets."

He had Victoria's full attention now.

"Would you be willing to tell me precisely what those secrets were?"

Fifteen

"My cousin loved mysteries," Mr Crookshaw continued. "She was fascinated by them, even when we were young she used to take us on treasure hunts around the grounds of her family home. She had all sorts of stories about the different areas of the garden. There was a ruined grotto she claimed held pearls left by a mermaid. Of course, that was childhood fantasy. As she got older, her tastes developed. The mysteries became more logical, but still curious."

"Did she have a particular interest in the mysteries of Bungay?" Victoria asked.

"Well, the legendary demon dog fascinated her and Baron Fitzhubert. She was working on something at the time of her death. We had been corresponding over the last few months of her life. My cousin knew she was dying, and she was trying to finish her last work before death overcame her. She was creating a work of fiction, within which she would reveal a secret that she had known about for a long time but had been too afraid to write about before."

"What sort of secret would she be afraid to reveal?"

"One that involved dangerous people, I presume," Crookshaw shrugged. "She never mentioned it in great detail in her letters. I assumed there must be a manuscript, or something left at the house, but I am not in a position to go there and look for it myself, and truth be told, I rather fancied this secret was the whimsy of an old lady who was in her declining months and craved something to distract her from her impending fate. I can understand that desire all too well."

"You blamed it on senility?" Victoria asked bluntly.

"I suppose you could say I did. After all, what sort of a secret could such a small town hold? I believe it had something to do with the castle ruins, as they were always her fascination. I started to feel that she had become too wrapped up in them. They had taken her away from the world, become an obsession for her. Sometimes, things like that happen. She had lost her husband a couple of years before and I knew she was lonely. She never had children and there was no close family around her. She was not one for making friends, either. Her world revolved around her stories."

"I didn't come across any manuscript for a new novel while I was at the house," Victoria said. "At least not in her writing cupboard."

"It's possible she hid it somewhere," Crookshaw replied. "If she was so concerned about its contents, that is. There was definitely an oddness in her letters, an indication that she was perhaps feeling harassed by someone. I put it down to her sickness."

Victoria didn't want to suggest that maybe Mrs Ward was not suffering from the effects of old age senility and that perhaps there was someone putting pressure on her, the same person who had been putting pressure on Mr Woolmer? But what secret could be so old and important to be worth intimidating an ageing writer over?

"How did your cousin die?" Victoria asked next.

Mr Crookshaw shrugged his shoulders.

"She was found one day, slumped over her typewriter. The doctors said it was her heart. As I said, she was ailing for some time."

"And what was in the typewriter when she passed?" Victoria pushed him.

Mr Crookshaw simply shook his head.

"I wasn't there. I only heard about it afterwards. I rarely leave the house and once I had inherited my late cousin's possessions I had my agent arrange for the cottage to be sold complete with its furniture. I did not care for the inconvenience of having it stripped first and the contents sold separately."

Victoria's mind was racing. Was she seeing a mystery where there was none? Or could there be more to the death of Mrs Ward that anybody imagined? Had she stumbled on a secret that had cost the lady her life?

As it was, they had gained all they could from Mr Crookshaw. Victoria asked a few more questions, but he was unable to offer anything else. He had not known his cousin that well in the last years of her life.

She finally thanked Mr Crookshaw for his time and bid him farewell before asking Lord Brooksby to take her back to Bungay.

"What is on your mind?" Brooksby asked her.

"Mr Crookshaw said his cousin was writing a book about a real secret just before she died."

"What sort of a secret? Something a person would kill for?" Brooksby said quietly.

He was thinking of his father.

"Well, there are lots of things that people will keep secret," Victoria remarked. "Money is a primary one. If the secret Mrs Ward knew held the key to great wealth or could ruin someone, that would be cause to kill people to avoid it being revealed. Then there is revenge, jealousy or someone desiring to hide up a past crime. There are lots of reasons why someone would become desperate to hide a secret and would do virtually anything to prevent the truth emerging."

They returned to the tower. There was still no sign of the workmen. Victoria asked Lord Brooksby about their absence.

"I agreed with Mr Dreary that work should be stopped until this matter is resolved. The death of Billy yesterday rather upset everybody deeply."

The carriage drew up outside the gates to the ruins. Victoria and Brooksby descended and headed back to the cottage. The door was still locked and there was no sign of Woolmer.

"We should make inquiries about your caretaker at some point. He can't possibly have gone far. He will hardly last long trying to shelter in the open this time of year. He's either found a place with someone around the town or he has retreated into the countryside to live off friends."

"As far as I am aware, he has no friends in this area and no family to speak of. But yes, you are right, I shall see to it that inquiries are made. I would not like to think of Mr Woolmer sleeping out in a ditch and dying from the cold. At least not until I know how he was involved in my father's death. I cannot believe he conspired to kill him."

Inside the cottage, Victoria went back to the cupboard where she had noticed all the papers. She began to empty it, to see if she had missed anything.

"Why did you ask what the last thing in the typewriter was?" Lord Brooksby enquired.

"I wondered if Mrs Ward was writing about her secret when she passed away and whether that paper had been left in the typewriter, or whether someone had taken it."

Lord Brooksby looked astonished.

"Your mind does certainly work in a very twisted and unexpected way. I never would have thought of something so dark and horrid."

"You start to see things differently when you are a detective for a while, or maybe I'm naturally suspicious," Victoria remarked.

She moved back to the little rosewood table and placed the papers down. There was not a lot of room, so she had to move the typewriter onto the floor. As she went through the papers again, there was nothing that shouted at her it was a precious secret. She found herself flipping back through the notes she had seen earlier.

"The only story here that could in any way be described as a secret is this one about the Bungay treasure," she said to Lord Brooksby, pointing out the very last page.

The article was brief. It talked about a rumour from the days of Baron Fitzhubert that a short time before he was executed for his treachery, he had hidden the family wealth. No one knew where it had gone, but there was a suspicion it had been buried somewhere in the grounds of the tower. Over the course of the succeeding centuries, various attempts had been made to uncover the treasure. Some said the baron had buried a box which contained vast amounts of gold coins and would make a man rich.

One scandalous attempt to find the treasure occurred in late 1817; five men went out in the dead of night and tried to dig up the grounds around the tower. This resulted in a good deal of consternation from the townsfolk, because the men were outsiders and if anybody were to get the treasure, it was surely meant to be the townspeople. When the men were spotted, a fight broke out on the grounds. However, the hole they had industriously excavated revealed nothing more than the forgotten burrows of a disused rabbit warren.

That had been the last major attempt to locate the treasure.

"It is a fiction," Lord Brooksby shook his head. "The sort of story you hear all across the county. I've heard of similar tales in many varied places. Surely you have too?"

"That is true," Victoria concurred. "There is the very famous mystery of King John's lost treasure in the Fens. No one has ever found that supposed hoard. And would a legendary, and probably fictitious treasure, be considered a secret that warranted people dying? I suppose we could argue that someone feared your workmen might stumble across the hoard and decided to take drastic action, but it doesn't seem likely."

Victoria paused for a minute, reading the story again.

"Of course it does tie in with that rumour Mr Hollobone mentioned about a secret dungeon beneath the castle. He said it is very odd that no one has ever located it."

"There is no dungeon beneath the tower. I know Mr Hollobone thinks that the castle ought to have one, that a man like Baron Fitzhubert would certainly have made good use of one. But just because we think one should exist doesn't mean it does."

"True, and after all this time, you would have thought someone would have stumbled across it. There ought to be an entryway somewhere."

Victoria found herself looking around the cottage again.

"When was this cottage built, Lord Brooksby?"

Brooksby considered for a moment.

"I don't know for sure, but I'm pretty certain it was somewhere around the 1500s."

"A few centuries after Baron Fitzhubert had passed and the tower had fallen into ruins," Victoria mused. "Plenty enough time for someone to find his secret dungeon unless he had somehow masked the entrance. Hidden it so well that no one would find it apart from him. Or someone to whom he had told the location."

"What are you getting at?" Lord Brooksby asked.

"This house doesn't have a cellar, does it?"

Lord Brooksby shook his head.

"Then that doesn't help us. A cellar might contain another secret doorway into the castle, much like the one upstairs. No cellar, but what other underground places could there be?"

Victoria glanced around her again, her eyes wandered into the kitchen.

"They wouldn't have had that water pump in the 1500s. The one that's over the sink."

"No, I believe there is an abandoned well somewhere behind the cottage," Brooksby responded. "It hasn't been used in quite some time. I think it was covered over and then the grass allowed to grow over and conceal it."

"A well," Victoria thought aloud. "A well that goes deep into the ground. I wonder how old it is? Might it have been here when the castle tower was built? They would have needed water to mix mortar and quench the workers' thirst. Castles always had wells."

Lord Brooksby merely shrugged at her helplessly.

"I am sorry Lord Brooksby. I'm going off on a tangent rather like my uncle does. In fact, I feel like I am channelling him right now. I sound just like Julius when he is off on one of his rambling speculations. I'm trying to see things that are probably not there."

"We are no closer to finding out who killed my father, are we?" Brooksby sighed, pulling a chair out from the table, and sitting down.

Victoria turned back to the typewriter that she had dropped onto the floor. She was thinking to herself about what she had wondered earlier. What was the last thing Mrs Ward had been writing? The paper was no longer in the typewriter. Maybe it was one of those she had found in the cupboard, or maybe it was something else, something worth killing over.

Had Mrs Ward been murdered too so she would not share the

secrets of this place?

If that were the case, the paper would be long gone, burned to ash in a fireplace no doubt. But there was another way she could find out what Mrs Ward had written if the paper thief had overlooked one small thing.

Victoria sat down by the typewriter and began to fumble around among the rollers that drew the paper through the machine. Catching her fingers a couple of times, and politely swearing under her breath, she eventually removed the long, inky ribbon that was used to print the letters upon the paper. Each time a letter key was pressed, and the corresponding letter stamped through the ribbon onto the paper, it left a negative in the ink. The ribbon was a record of everything that had been written on the typewriter and it was possible to read what had been lost by examining the ribbon. At least, that was her theory.

Brooksby watched her in silence as she unravelled the ribbon and held it up to the dimming light, her fingers swiftly becoming covered in ink.

"What are you doing?"

"If I read out these letters, could you write them on a piece of paper for me?" Victoria asked Brooksby without answering his query.

Brooksby simply nodded his head and retrieved a piece of paper and a pencil. Tentatively, Victoria began to read out the letters from the ribbon. By necessity she was working backwards through the sentences imprinted in negative as she unravelled the ribbon. The story she began to reveal was not what she had expected. The very last document that Mrs Ward had typed was not a story revealing secrets.

At least not in the way that Victoria had expected.

She found she was reading what was essentially Ethel Ward's suicide note.

When all the words were down on the piece of paper, Lord

Brooksby stared at them. His face had gone a fraction pale.

Ethel Ward had written that she was in a great deal of pain. She was tired of life, tired of living in grief for her late husband, and she wished to depart from this existence as gracefully as possible. She wrote that she had taken an overdose of sleeping pills just before she sat down to type her last letter, and she anticipated her end would come swiftly. In fact, it seemed she had not quite finished typing her letter as the drugs had taken over and she had slumped onto her typewriter. There was no mention of a secret. Just the sad story of a woman who was at the end of her days and could not face her ongoing suffering.

Right to the very end, Ethel Ward had kept her true secrets to herself. They would never know if she had someone else living at the property, someone who used the upstairs rooms and who she would not reveal to anyone. Someone who knew about the secret door onto the tower battlements. And what other secrets had she been supposedly keeping hidden from Crookshaw?

"Did he get it wrong?" Brooksby said. "When he said Ethel had found out one final, dramatic secret, one she was going to write about in her novel, he thought it meant something about Bungay. But maybe the true secret was that Ethel Ward had grown tired of life. That she was planning to do away with herself."

Victoria put down the typewriter ribbon. Her fingers were stained black with ink. She felt somewhat despondent. They were no closer to the killer and all they had discovered was that Ethel Ward had been a sad figure in her last days. Alone, ill and frightened for the future, she had come to the conclusion that she had to take action herself.

Victoria sat on a chair opposite Lord Brooksby.

"You are disappointed," Lord Brooksby observed. "You were convinced you would find the key to this mystery on that typewriter ribbon."

"I suppose I am disappointed. I really thought I had found the solution. I am not finished though, Lord Brooksby. There is a great deal more to discover as yet and I won't let you down."

Brooksby simply nodded his head.

"There is a part of me that deeply regrets getting anyone involved in this saga," he murmured. "I should have known better. I should never have tried to make this place what my father desired. I should have left it as a ruin."

"None of this is your fault, Lord Brooksby. Billy's death is not your responsibility. It's all due to the villain who has been targeting people here."

But I could have protected the workmen better instead of encouraging them to keep going on, telling them to forget about the stories and what they had seen. I could have sent them home until you had concluded your investigation."

"As my uncle told you, we didn't want you to do that. We wanted you to stand up tall before this evil person to show you are not intimidated. Therefore, we must shoulder our share of this burden of regret too. We are just as responsible as anybody else for the death of Billy."

Lord Brooksby didn't seem to be listening to her, nothing she said could make him feel better.

"My dear, if you are done here, I rather would like to get home I am feeling rather jaded."

"I ought to check on my uncle," Victoria agreed. "We shall lock up the house once more."

She glanced at the papers around her and decided at the last moment to take both Ethel's notes and the typewriter ribbon so that she could show them to her uncle.

Unfortunately, her fingers were now covered in ink, and she didn't want to touch the papers and smear them too. She went looking for a spare piece of paper that she could tuck the others inside, to protect them as she carried them. The cupboard was now empty, but there were drawers beneath it.

Using her handkerchief so as not to spread ink everywhere, she pulled the drawers open and discovered a bundle of larger pieces of paper within. Perhaps these were sheets that Ethel Ward had been intending to cut up to fit in the typewriter. She pulled one out that was folded in half and would fit over the notes perfectly. She unfolded the paper in readiness to place the notes and ribbon inside and, as she did so, was startled into amazement by what she found on the reverse of the folded paper.

"Look at this, Lord Brooksby!"

Brooksby had been heading towards the door, now he turned back around to see what she had found.

"What is it?" He asked.

Victoria was scanning her gaze across the papers.

"These are architectural plans," she said. "Old architectural plans. Someone drew these of the castle ruins and the cottage beside it. And here is the well, but more to the point, look at this."

Victoria's pointing finger drew Brooksby's attention. Upon the paper, drawn in dashed lines to indicate it was not visible above the surface, was what appeared to be a short tunnel. It did not lead from the well, as Victoria had first expected, but veered off from the tower at an angle away from them. Fascinatingly, there was an indication of stairs leading down to it, though the ink outlining them on the plans had faded badly.

"I think we just found the route to the secret dungeon," Victoria said in elation. "Ethel Ward knew more than we realised."

Sixteen

Victoria was torn between looking for the secret entrance immediately or heading back to her uncle with this information first. She knew full well that Bainbridge would want to be in on this and would be most aggrieved if she found the secret dungeon without him. Even so, the thought of having to abandon her quest right at the moment when she had found the key to the mystery in these plans was almost unbearable.

After considering everything for a while, her conscience got the better of her and she decided to go back to Bainbridge first. It simply wouldn't be fair otherwise. Not to mention it was getting dark and gloomy outside. Not the ideal time to look for secret underground passages.

They would need equipment to help them. Lanterns and possibly an extra pair of hands. The thought of going into a secret dungeon alone when there could be a killer lurking nearby did not strike Victoria as a good idea. She very much doubted that Lord Brooksby would be much help if they were attacked. She could quite imagine him running away the second any danger arose and leaving her to it.

Her mind made-up, Victoria explained to Lord Brooksby her plans and he kindly offered to drop her outside the inn, which would mean she avoided getting any wetter than she already was.

She arrived at the inn just in time for dinner and found Bainbridge comfortably tucked up in his bed with a tray of food before him. Dinner appeared to consist of some sort of stew. There was a great quantity of beef and potatoes and two bread rolls to dunk into the thick gravy. Bainbridge looked quite content, especially as there was a tankard of beer to accompany his meal.

Victoria was relieved to see he was looking an awful lot healthier too. The colour had returned to his face and his smile was back. When she asked him if he still felt feverish, he remarked that his symptoms were much improved.

"And what have you been up to?"

Victoria placed the papers she had brought with her onto the bed, along with the plans that she had folded them up in. She had found a second piece of paper, this one blank, which she had carefully wrapped around the ink ribbon so it wouldn't damage anything. She began to show Bainbridge all the different documents; the original manuscript for Ethel Ward's novel, her notes on the various secrets around the town, including the supposedly lost Bungay treasure, and then the typewriter ribbon. She explained the story of how Ethel Ward had been found slumped over her typewriter, but that there had been no paper within it.

"It seemed to me that someone decided to remove her suicide note."

"That seems a very logical conclusion," Bainbridge concurred. "It could have been whoever found her and didn't wish for her death to be noted as a suicide. There is such a stigma about such things. Without the note, it could have been supposed that she had taken one too many of her sleeping powders in her frail condition, ailing as she was. It could be seen as an accident."

"Precisely. I don't see any reason to consider it suspicious as such.

Initially, I almost wondered if Ethel Ward had been murdered because she was intending to write about this secret she knew in her latest novel. But I'm not convinced that was the case. I think things have been muddled up together. On the one hand, she was tracking down all the legends of lost treasures and ghosts in the town before her death, perhaps planning to use them in another novel. But she was also aware of her secret plans to do away with herself, and this was what she mentioned to her cousin. She could not come out directly and tell him what she was thinking, so she hinted at it. Perhaps, as he was the only person she had to write to, she felt it was fitting she confide in him.

"And then, of course, 20 years have passed. In that time, many things get confused. People forget things or combine information to come up with new ideas. Yes, it is entirely reasonable to suppose that her cousin has convoluted the two notions and come up with something entirely novel.

"However, that doesn't change the fact that Ethel Ward *did* know about a secret concerning the tower. I am not sure exactly when she came upon these plans or who designed them, but if you look at them, you can see there is marked what appears to be a secret entrance or tunnel."

Bainbridge took the plans off Victoria and cast his eyes over them. He traced his finger along the line of the secret tunnel that was marked by the dashes on the paper.

"Well, well, it seems Mr Hollobone was onto something after all. Except he did not have access to these plans."

"The entrance appears to be some way from the tower," Victoria added, pointing at the diagram. "My surmise is that it's been covered up in some way that makes it almost impossible to see unless you know it is there. Yet someone has presumably found it."

"Why do you say that?" Bainbridge asked.

"Because I think the person who has been causing all these problems at the tower site, who caused the death of the late Lord Brooksby and now poor Billy, knows about the secret dungeon and what it contains. And he doesn't want anybody else getting access to it."

"That is an interesting conclusion, but let's extrapolate on this a bit more. If someone discovered the route to a secret dungeon beneath the tower, then the first thing they would do would be to explore the place, and if there was some treasure down there, it would no doubt be portable. They could therefore remove it any time they pleased. If we are supposing this person has been hanging around the tower for years, based on what you have learned about Mrs Ethel Ward not liking people going upstairs in her home, then they must be incredibly inefficient treasure hunters. Why has it taken them so long to remove the treasure?"

Victoria paused. Her uncle was right. It would be easy for anybody who knew about the dungeon and its contents to simply steal away everything as soon as they could. They could have done it when the cottage was empty. Why would they still be hanging around if that were their intention?

"I do believe you are onto something," Bainbridge tried to cheer his niece as she looked disappointed that her theory had been so easily quashed. "What I am wondering is whether this dungeon contains something that cannot be easily moved. That would imply it's something that is routinely replenished, or something that is of such permanence it simply cannot be taken elsewhere."

"But what would that be?" Victoria frowned.

"The obvious answer that springs to mind is that something down in those dungeons would reveal a crime that happened years ago, such as a murder. One possibility is a grave was dug down there and a body deposited. For whatever reason, it may be simply impossible to recover the body easily by the person responsible and they are now in a position where they are scared someone else will discover it and realised what they did."

"That would not explain why someone was living secretly in Ethel Ward's house all those years," Victoria shook her head.

"It was but one theory. There could be many others. My point is our next stage is to get into this secret passageway. However, we must not do it alone, Vicky. Someone out there is a dangerous killer, and they will do virtually anything to prevent people finding out the truth. Right at this moment, they're banking on people believing there is a murderous phantom lurking around the tower to keep their secret safe, but if they realised we have worked out where their hideout is, they may choose to take drastic action to ensure their secret remains hidden."

"What do you propose we do?"

"You have already stated much of the solution yourself. We need to recruit a party of people and find this tunnel in the morning. I suggest Mr Hollobone is involved. He certainly would be glad to know his theories were correct. But we should also see if we can encourage the workmen from Lord Brooksby's team to come with us. We don't know what we might find. There could be stones or other devices that need to be moved to allow us access and, let's be blunt, it would be advisable to have some burly men with us for the sake of protection."

It was exactly what Victoria had been thinking earlier. Going into the tunnel by herself at night would have been simply stupid when she didn't know if the killer was lurking inside, having fled there after they had found his secret room.

"I believe tomorrow morning will reveal the solution to this puzzle. Though it may not give us the means to apprehend the murderer,"

Bainbridge persisted. "However, we shall be closer to knowing the *why* behind this terrible series of events, and once you know the why, the *who* becomes easier."

"Do you think you will be well enough to come tomorrow?"

Bainbridge smiled at her.

"I am determined to be well enough. Nothing stops me from exploring old and ancient hidden tunnels. This is just the sort of case I love."

Satisfied that her uncle seemed a good deal better, Victoria left him alone and went downstairs to speak to Mr Savage about making preparations for the next day. She wanted to know how to contact Mr Hollobone and to send a note to Lord Brooksby asking him if he could get his workmen to come to the tower. She hoped that at the very least they would be prepared to come if it meant catching the killer who had taken out one of their number.

Her arrangements made, she settled down to a meal in the taproom at the back of the inn and enjoyed a solitary feast of beef and potatoes while sitting by the fire, warming herself through. She felt a sense of comfort and ease. Her body relaxed, some of the tension from the day lifting. They were closer to resolving this mystery. They were closer to a solution. Sooner rather than later, they would know the full story of this matter.

When the next day dawned, they found that the weather gods had been kindly to them. There was a frail sun beaming from the sky and, as the early morning mist gradually dispersed, they saw it was going to be a bright, if cold, day. Just the sort for exploring ancient tunnels.

Bainbridge felt very sprightly as he dressed in his finest tweed suit, with his stout walking stick to hand. He made sure his boots were tightly laced up and had an extra pair of socks on his feet to keep them warm and dry. He also had a hip flask of whisky in his pocket, ready just in case he felt the last dregs of his cold returning.

Amazing how the prospect of exploring an ancient tunnel and solving a mystery could eradicate his cold better than all the pills and potions a doctor could prescribe him. He headed downstairs to meet up with the rest of their party.

Mr Hollobone had received Victoria's note the night before, explaining that she at last knew where the secret tunnel to the dungeon was. He had been barely able to contain his excitement, almost rushing over to the inn the second he had read her missive. Sleep had been impossible after that and, instead, he had spent most of the night scouring through his books for any information that could be useful to them. He was bleary eyed when he arrived at the inn, but full of enthusiasm for the hunt.

Dressed in his best walking outfit and with stout shoes that would rival Bainbridge's rugged boots, he had also brought a lantern and a three-foot wooden ruler to help them work out the depth and distance of the tunnel. As a keen amateur cartographer he was fully prepared to chart the tunnel and was well-supplied with a satchel of paper and pencils slung over his shoulder.

Victoria showed him the plans that she had found in Ethel Ward's home. He studied them eagerly, ashamed he had never discovered them before. Hollobone prided himself on being the best historian in the town, yet somehow he had failed to locate these plans. He was abashed at his failure.

"I wonder how accurate they are," he mumbled as he studied the plans. "It may require a little bit of assumption to help us find the exact entranceway. There doesn't appear to be a scale on these plans. They're more a rudimentary guide."

"They give us a starting point and that is all we need," Victoria smiled at him.

"That is very true, young lady. I am most excited for this venture."

Just before nine, the workmen arrived at the inn. They looked somewhat sheepish as they headed through the door. The inn was of a slightly higher class than what they were used to, and they would not normally venture into such a place. It was a coaching inn designed for well-to-do travellers, not for the working classes. Mr Dreary led his crew uneasily inside.

"Mr Dreary, I am delighted that you could join us," Bainbridge spoke to him the second he was in the room.

"The message we received was rather cryptic. It seemed prudent for us to come," Dreary responded. "We owe it to Billy to try and find out who did this."

Bainbridge had hoped this would be his response. In fact, he had banked on it to ensure that the workmen turned up.

"Now we are all present, I suggest we make our way to the tower. We don't have much daylight ahead of us and this could take some time," Bainbridge addressed them all with a smile on his face before he led them out of the inn.

They headed as a group towards the tower. The gates stood open, and Lord Brooksby's carriage was just arriving. Victoria had explained as much detail as she could in her note to him the night before, instructing him to do all he could to have his workmen appear at the inn. She had not expected to see him in person after their conversation the day before. She had rather imagined that he would be too uneasy about the whole situation to appear. She had underestimated him, she realised. She was prone to doing that, especially with men.

She was pleased to see she had been wrong and Brooksby was determined to see through this matter and bring justice to his father and the unfortunate Billy.

Lord Brooksby acknowledged their arrival with a polite nod as they appeared at the gates.

"We have placed Mr Hollobone in charge of deciphering the plans," Bainbridge explained to him. "He seems best suited to such a task."

Mr Hollobone was delighted to be in charge of the plans. He had brought a compass with him and was now using it to try and decipher exactly where they should branch off from the main circular base of the tower to follow the tunnel marked on the map and, hopefully, find its entrance. Before he was allowed to start, however, they determined that they would initially make sure there was no one lurking up on the battlements. Victoria had explained to the workmen as they were travelling, how someone had used the secret doorway to slip up to the top of the tower and throw stones down at those below. Mr Dreary and his crew were eager to check out these battlements for themselves, and if there was any sign of someone up there, they would be quick to grab him. Unlocking the door to Mr Woolmer's cottage, she took them upstairs and through the secret room and up to the passage that led to the top of the tower. She was not expecting anybody to be there – the cottage had been locked up and it would be somewhat foolish, now that the secret had been revealed for, the 'phantom' to hang around up on the battlements, even if they could find a way passed the locked door. Even so, it was just as well to be safe.

A swift search of the battlements revealed them to be empty to the satisfaction of everybody. They could now continue with the rest of their mission without fear of thrown objects. Mr Dreary was bemused that someone had been using a secret doorway to stand on the battlements and peer down at them all this time.

"When the lads kept telling me they had seen someone up on the ruins, I didn't believe them. I thought they were just being superstitious."

He explained to Victoria as they moved back downstairs.

"It was a perfectly natural assumption," Victoria responded. "Why should there be anyone up on the ruins after all? Easy enough on a dull or dark day for someone to mistake something else for a shadowy figure wandering the tower."

"I should have paid more heed," Mr Dreary shook his head, refusing to be consoled. "If I had, then perhaps Billy would not be dead."

"That was hardly your fault. You do not deserve to bear guilt or responsibility for what happened to him. The only person who is guilty here is the one who was throwing masonry down from the tower top in a deliberate attempt to hurt others."

Mr Dreary shook his head. It would take a lot more than kind words from Victoria to convince him that he bore no guilt for the loss of the young workman. Billy's death would haunt him to the end of his own days. He would always wonder, if he had done things slightly differently, if he had listened to his men instead of telling them to be quiet and not pay heed to ghost stories, if perhaps the young man would still be with them.

They rejoined the others at the bottom of the tower. Hollobone was standing just behind the cottage. He had already worked out roughly the direction they needed to walk in to reach where he presumed the entrance to the tower was. He was raring to go, almost jumping up and down on the spot. Bainbridge looked just as eager. He took a sip from his hip flask seeming fully rejuvenated after his recent indisposition and keen to start.

"You take the lead, Mr Hollobone," he instructed the man.

Hollobone needed no further permission or encouragement. He checked his compass one last time then, with a sharp thrust of his stick ahead of him, he gave the command to move off.

"Follow me!"

Then he was on the march, and they were all following him and waiting patiently to see what would be at the end of their quest.

Seventeen

Mr Hollobone marched them across the open ground with confidence. They had not gone very far when he started to tap the ground with his stick.

"What is he doing?" Victoria asked her uncle.

"I believe he is trying to work out if he can hear the hollow space beneath the ground of a tunnel and I very much doubt he will succeed."

Bainbridge appeared to be correct because, after a few paces, Mr Hollobone stopped with this endeavour and instead focused on walking forward. They were coming to the edge of the land that surrounded the ruined tower, where an old wall belonging to a neighbouring property cut across and divided the landscape. There was a great deal of brambles encasing the wall, along with other dense wild plants that created a further barrier. Mr Hollobone had taken rough measurements from the plans, and now, as he marched towards the wall, his eyebrows lifted, and he paused.

"By my calculations, the tunnel runs under that wall and the entrance would be beyond it."

He pointed his stick at the brick wall. It looked ancient, parts of it contained flint work and it had the haphazard appearance of something that had been built and expanded over numerous years. As they drew closer, and the workmen began to pull away some of the brambles, it became apparent that its base was made of similar stonework to the tower. It might even have been put up around the same time, or at the very least stones from the ruined tower had been repurposed to construct it.

However, there was no sign of an entranceway to a tunnel. The ground ran directly up to the wall and stopped.

"What is on the other side of this wall?" Bainbridge asked Lord Brooksby.

"I believe this backs on to some stables," Brooksby explained. "And there is a blacksmith's workshop just around the corner. If I'm thinking correctly, that might abut at a right angle onto this wall."

"Yes, he is quite correct," Hollobone announced. "The entranceway must be within the blacksmith's workshop or his stables, and what a convenient way to hide it! As long as those in the smithy were in on the secret, of course."

Since they could not pursue the tunnel through the wall, they headed back out to the gates and journeyed around the winding streets until they came to the smithy. Mr Hollobone continued to take measurements using his compass and ruler, until he was satisfied that they were in exactly the spot they needed to be. They entered the yard of the smithy, and Hollobone pointed to a line of stable stalls where he proposed the entrance to the secret tunnel could be found.

They were being watched by the smithy working at his forge as they milled about the yard and took a good look at the stables. Like many smithing workshops the front of his premises was open to allow the heat from his forge to escape. Even on a cold day in winter, the smith would drip with sweat as he worked. Now, he could easily see his strange new customers wandering about his yard.

He was currently making repairs to a garden spade while his two apprentices were working in the background. He paused and watched what these strangers were doing, a frown crossing his brow.

Already a big and burly man before years of smithing had built extra muscle and brought strength to his arms, he was not a man you wanted to get on the wrong side of. He watched the strange party of people traipse over to the stables, which currently held two equine residents waiting to be shod. Wondering what was going on, he abandoned his work on the spade and headed over to demand to know what these new visitors wanted.

One of them had a large piece of paper in his hands that he kept referring to, flicking his attention between it and the stables. He kept saying something along the lines of – "it should be around here, somewhere."

At least one of the party was a wealthy gentleman. The smith had a vague idea who Lord Brooksby was, his coachman having once brought in a horse which had lost its shoe when they had travelled into the town. Aside from that, he didn't have much to do with what was going on at the tower beyond his back wall. Why would he? The tower had always been there since he was a lad. He had looked at it from a distance many times. But he had no real interest in it and, unlike some of the townsfolk, he had no reason to walk past it on a regular occasion. He had heard people moaning about the fact that it was being fenced off and they would not be allowed to cut across the grounds anymore, but that hardly caused him any concern. He was the sort of fellow who felt that if something didn't concern him directly, it was not worth getting involved in.

"Hey, what are you lot up to?" He demanded of the nearest man, who happened to be Mr Dreary.

The smith wasn't prepared to confront his lordship with such a demand, but a workman was fair game, and he was quite prepared to accost him and demand to know what all this nonsense was about. Mr Dreary turned around, opening his mouth to attempt to explain, when Bainbridge rapidly interceded.

"Good morning to you. We're looking for the entranceway to a secret tunnel that runs underneath the tower next door. We believe it might be in one of your stable stalls."

The blacksmith was thrown by this information.

"A secret passage," he said. "Never heard of the like."

"But as you can see, the plans I have here clearly show that the tunnel is supposed to run in this direction, and from the measurements I have taken, it must come out in one of your stables."

Mr Hollobone showed him the plans and pointed out exactly what he meant by the tunnel running into the stables.

The blacksmith studied them for a moment, scratching at his head.

"My stables all have solid floors," he told them. "I wouldn't have some opening in the floor in case a horse could fall down it."

"But what about that stall?"

Victoria pointed to the stall that was on the far end of the stables and that didn't appear to have any room in it for a horse. It was stacked with various items; long lengths of wood, piles of rope, even some barrels.

"That?" The smith stared at the space. "I use that as storage space. The only thing in it is the remains of a dried up well. I couldn't tell you the last time anyone used it. When my father took on this smithy, he had a new well dug behind the forge. The old one is covered with a stout lid to prevent anybody falling into it."

They were all immediately intrigued. Victoria cast a look at Lord Brooksby, triumphant that her theory about a disused well being the source of the secret tunnel was proving correct – even if she had initially chosen the wrong well to be the entrance.

"I would like to take a look at that well," Bainbridge said, moving to the stall to peer inside.

"You can't get in it easy," the smith folded his arms across his massive chest and glared at them as they were infuriating troublemakers. "It has a bolt on it which must be rusted to heck by now. It hasn't been lifted in donkeys' years. I wouldn't allow it and what would be the point?"

"You mean to say that no one else comes into this stall?" Victoria asked him.

"Why would they?"

The smith was now sorely confused by the situation.

"I take it you do not reside here at the smithy?" Bainbridge interjected.

"No, I do not. I have a house a few streets away."

"Is there anyone on site overnight?"

"Only the old man," the smith shrugged. "His name is Ernest. He's been tending the horses for the smithy for as long as I can remember. Real old salt of the earth. He didn't have anywhere to go, so he sleeps above the horses in the stables at night and watches over the place to make sure no one comes in to try and steal anything."

"And he has been here a very long time, perhaps longer than twenty years?" Bainbridge asked.

"He started here not long after my father took over the smithy. It had been left to go to ruin by the previous owner. They hadn't found anybody to take it on until my father came along. Ernest walked in one day and asked if there might be work for someone who was good with horses. He was a young man then, of course. My father tried him out. Liked how we handled the animals and was agreeable to him becoming his horseman. Part of the agreement was that Ernest would sleep above the stables. It gave him a roof over his head and gave us extra security at night. Why are you interested in that?"

Victoria had stopped listening. She had already opened the door to the stall and was heading inside. It was necessary to move various items out of her way; a coil of rope was inconveniently placed just inside the door and some long planks of wood blocked her view. With assistance from the workmen, it did not take long to sort through the detritus stored in the stall and reveal the old well. In fact, it almost seemed as if the items blocking the well, though they appeared placed inside in a haphazard manner, were really very carefully arranged to make it relatively easy to remove them. And, despite what the smith had said, the bolt holding the well cover in place was clearly well oiled and far from rusty. The wood of the trapdoor was solid, not a sign of rot in it. She shot back the bolt and lifted up the lid.

The blacksmith was clearly astonished when he heard the bolt slide easily across and the lid lift up. He moved forward to stare into the stall.

"What are you doing?"

"Down there is an entrance to an old and ancient tunnel that leads beneath the tower," Victoria told him firmly. "At least that is our theory."

Mr Dreary now handed her a lamp that he had lit, and she held it over the mouth of the well.

"If we were to get a length of rope and use Mr Hollobone's measuring stick to make knots along its length at set widths, we could then work out how deep this well is," she suggested.

It was an old yet reliable trick. With the smith's permission, they set to work making a measuring rope. They used an old horseshoe at one end to weight it so they would be able to know when it touched the bottom, and they set the knots at equal distances of a foot each. Once they were done, Mr Dreary came to the edge of the hole and gradually began to play out the rope down into the darkness.

Victoria was counting out the knots, watching them as they went down. When they got to ten feet she began to wonder if they were chasing their tails again. Could that old map really be pointing them towards this forgotten well? Mr Dreary continued to play out the rope; before he had quite reached fifteen feet the horseshoe clunked on the bottom of the dry well.

"Your old well does not seem to be particularly deep," Bainbridge remarked to the smith. "You wouldn't get much water from that."

The smith was looking more and more confused. If the well were not deep enough to provide water why was it there?

Having determined the depth of the well, it became apparent to Dreary and the other workmen that it would be difficult to get down using the rope alone. Dreary sent back his lads to fetch his longest ladder, though he was not sure it would be sufficient. His lads had thought the same and returned a moment later, not only with the longest ladder but with a second, shorter one. Their suggestion was to firmly tie one ladder to the other. Thus making a ladder that was over fifteen feet in length.

Victoria was now looking down the hole, feeling slightly apprehensive. She wasn't sure if she wanted to climb down into that dark space using the rickety pair of ladders. Her sense of self-preservation was beginning to override her sense of curiosity.

Bainbridge, however, was eager to get going. He'd already made a brief assessment of the well mouth to work out whether his girth would fit through the narrow opening and was satisfied that he would have just about enough room. Victoria did not share his sense of adventure and, though it took all her powers of persuasion, she convinced him to allow someone else to enter the shaft first –

specifically one of the workmen.

Two workmen volunteered for the task, looking as if they anticipated finding a pot of gold at the bottom of the well. They were both nimble enough and sprightly enough to shimmy down the ladder with ease. If their discovery proved to be just that – a dried-up well – and there was no entrance way into the secret tunnel, then there was no point anybody else climbing down. In particular, there would be no point her uncle puffing and panting his way down.

Matt was selected as the first volunteer to head down the well. He took the lamp off Victoria and clambered down the first ladder without any concerns about the possibility of the knots holding the two together coming apart.

He reached the bottom in moments, and they heard him jumping off the ladder and onto the ground with a thud. He held up the lamp and it glowed in the base of the well, illuminating him as they peered down from the surface.

"What do you see?" Mr Hollobone asked anxiously.

"There's a doorway, alright," Matt called up to them. "Just like the one we saw leading out from the cottage and on to the battlements."

Victoria had hardly dared to breathe as Matt had clambered down, her anticipation like a lump in her stomach as she hoped that they would be correct in finding the tunnel entrance in the base of the well. The whole idea had seemed preposterous until the moment Matt had revealed it was the truth.

The blacksmith was still edging around them, utterly baffled by what was going on.

"You have never used this well, or this stall, I take it?" Bainbridge asked him.

"Only for storage. And truth be told, it's Ernest who tends to look after that part of things. If you tell him to tidy up the ropes or harnesses or anything like that, he's the one who sorts it and puts it away."

It was slowly dawning on the blacksmith that if Ernest was the one going in and out of this stall, then he also must be the one who knew about the lid to the well. Someone had to have made sure that bolt was well oiled and that the lid was easily accessible at all times. He was becoming troubled by the thought of a secret right beneath his feet that he knew nothing about.

"What is all this?"

"We shall get to that in a moment, first of all, we need to know exactly what is down in that tunnel," Bainbridge replied.

There was now a short discussion about who would go down the well next. Matt relayed from his position at the bottom that the tunnel itself appeared quite narrow but was tall enough for a man to walk through and at some point had been shored up with woodwork. Despite how well maintained it appeared, it remained a tight space, and the air inside it smelt stale. Mr Hollobone explained to them how the deeper underground you got, the worse the air would be, and a tunnel could only be so long before the air became completely stagnant and impossible to breathe.

"It is why they have to pump air into deep tunnels in mines," Hollobone explained. "Or provide an air shaft."

"This is not an adventure designed for you," Victoria said gently to her uncle. "I think it would be best if you remained at the top and Mr Dreary sent down his workmen. They're all nimble and used to these sorts of things. Everyone must also be extremely careful and keep an eye on each other. If anyone feels faint or dizzy, they ought to come out at once."

Bainbridge was deeply disappointed. Still, when he considered his size, age and not to mention his recent bad cold, he admitted to himself he was not the fellow to go down the well. Reluctantly, he agreed to allow Mr Dreary's workmen to take on the task. Matt was eager enough. He had already explored a short portion of the tunnel and noted that it got wider as you went on.

"It don't seem to be that long," he remarked to his fellows.

That was logical enough, as their route from the tower to the smithy had not taken them very far. The tower was only a short distance beyond the wall.

"I imagine at some point they intended to link this entrance way to another building," Mr Hollobone was drawing on a fresh piece of paper. "Looking at some of the stonework of this old structure, I half wonder if this was part of something to do with the castle at some point. The intention could easily have been to create a bigger cellar and a passageway that led directly to the tower, an easy way to get in and out and as we've decided before, to hide a dungeon. Dungeons were always designed to be gloomy, claustrophobic spaces, the sort of place you could dump somebody and forget about them."

Victoria shuddered. Her mind flicked to all the things that could be at the end of that tunnel, most of them unpleasant. If there was a dungeon, what if someone had been left down there to die and be forgotten about? Her imagination had been well-fuelled by Gothic novels and reading through Bainbridge's archives on criminal cases, and it could summon up all manner of grisly sights without effort.

She didn't relay any of this information to the men around her, as she didn't want the workmen to be spooked. Two others now joined Matt in the well, all with lanterns, and they headed into the gloomy tunnel. It was not long before they called back, saying that someone had been down there recently making sure the walls were shored up with new woodwork to ensure the roof could not fall in. Then they fell into silence.

They had gone too far down the tunnel for those on the surface to hear them.

"Most secret tunnel stories are complete nonsense, you know," Hollobone chatted as they waited for the men to return. "It's simply impractical to build something of that length. You have to consider all the work that has to go into it. Mines don't simply spring up overnight and the amount of effort required it is going to be noticed by people. But, at the same time, it is entirely feasible to create small, short tunnels underground without people being aware."

They waited impatiently for news from below. As the time drifted on, they started to wonder if the workmen were in trouble. The blacksmith tapped his foot on the ground, folded his arms and looked agitated.

"What if they don't make it out?" He said to them.

No one wanted to think along those lines. The last thing any of them needed was for the workmen to get trapped beneath the ground and be unable to return.

"They should be perfectly fine," Victoria told him sharply.

The blacksmith cast her a disbelieving look, but he said no more. As the sun drifted across the sky and a cold shadow fell across them, they grew more and more worried about the men they had sent down. Then, just as they were about to panic and think they might have to send a rescue party, they heard the rushing of feet. Matt reappeared at the base of the tunnel.

"What have you found?" Dreary called out to him.

"Treasure!" Matt shouted back. "Barrels and barrels of it."

He held something up in his hands, it was a small barrel with its lid open. They couldn't see the contents contained within clearly from that distance.

"Bring it up here," Dreary demanded of him.

Matt scrabbled for the ladder and clambered up to the surface with one hand on the rungs, while the other clung to the small barrel. When he reached the surface, he handed the barrel to his employer.

"There's tonnes of this stuff down there. There's a big old empty room beneath the tower foundations. There must be some tiny slit windows, or something, cut into lower walls, because there were little chinks of light and air coming into the room."

Dreary took the barrel and examined the dark contents. What he discovered inside was a great quantity of tobacco.

"Well now," Bainbridge said, looking at the barrel. "At least we now have an idea of what is going on here. Tobacco is just one substance that is the stock in trade for a smuggler."

"Smuggling!" Dreary looked astonished.

"Admittedly, we are not close to the coast, but that's not the point. Smuggling doesn't just occur near the sea. It requires someone in land to move the stuff on. That is what is happening here. The smugglers bring their stock to Bungay, hide it in this secret dungeon and then, at a suitable time, move it on again. This is the perfect place. No one knows about it, except, I think we can agree, one person."

"I don't know anything," the blacksmith said hastily. "I would never get involved in smuggling."

"I was not referring to you," Bainbridge smiled at him. "But I was referring to someone who you know very well."

Eighteen

Ernest had had a bad night with his rheumatism. These days he was lucky if he got a full night's sleep at the best of times. More often he tossed and turned, his ankles swollen, his toes and fingers throbbing. A long life of hard work had left him with these woes, and the fact he slept above a stable in a pile of straw, just as he had done all his life, did not aid things. If there were horses beneath him, the warmth that drifted up from their bodies at least kept him fairly comfortable. At other times, he was reliant on his flimsy blanket and the thin mattress he laid upon.

Other men would have tried to improve their lot. They would have tried to find a home. Maybe even got married. But Ernest had always known that this was to be his place. From the day he had asked for a job here he had known that this was where he would live and where he would die. He had never had any ambition beyond it. He was chained to this place both because of his lack of ambition and because he felt a care of duty to the smith whose father had first provided him with the opportunity. Ernest was lacking in many things, but he was not lacking in loyalty.

He hadn't moved from his mattress as he heard the commotion down below. The upper floor of the stables was not enclosed, one side was fully open to the stalls just below and there was a ladder that led down from Ernest's aerie.

He had heard everything that was going on downstairs. He could have left at any moment and avoided the questions that were bound to come his way. He could have clambered down the ladder and simply disappeared. He might even have climbed out of one of the windows that had been installed in either side of his sleeping space to provide light. But he didn't moved. Truth be told, he was tired of all these games. He was tired of his role in this strange saga that had now led to bloodshed.

Ernest was not a killer. He had never wished to see anybody suffer harm. He had simply been trying to keep out of trouble and had found himself stuck between a rock and hard place. Things had gone too far, and he could not deal with the guilt that had brought. He felt indirectly responsible for the deaths at the tower.

When he heard his name being called, he gradually heaved himself off the mattress. That was the other reason he hadn't moved, of course; his body was so stiff and sore the thought of running had not appealed. He hobbled over to the ladder, wondering if his aching feet could even manage to carry him down it.

"Yes, Master Smith?" He called down.

"Please come down at once, Ernest. We need to talk."

Ernest eased himself onto the ladder. His fingers did not want to bend to grip the rungs. His feet protested as they slipped onto the slats. He hobbled down, a crooked and broken old man. When he was finally on the floor, everything ached, and he shivered in the cold.

The first thing he saw was sympathy in the eyes of a man he did not recognise. The gentleman was obesely fat. Ernest had never even dreamt of being that large. The thought of having enough food to enable a person to reach such a size had never crossed his mind. The man had a kindly face, however, and he looked at Ernest in a way many did not.

"I think this fellow needs to be sitting beside your fire," he told the smith with an edge to his tone.

Mr Fenton was the name of the smith, and he was, in general, not a kindly man towards his employees. That wasn't to say he was abusive or cruel. He simply didn't pay them much consideration. He wanted them to just get on with the tasks he assigned them so his business would continue. It was why he had never considered the fact that he was forcing an elderly man to sleep above the stables. After so many years of good service, another employer might have reasoned that it was about time Ernest had a better place to sleep, especially now his rheumatism was causing him to struggle to get up and down the ladder.

Mr Fenton simply didn't understand. He didn't see things that were not explained to him. He just carried on in his narrow world of routine and work as he had always done. Now he tried to grasp at what Bainbridge was suggesting. Finally, he agreed they should all go back into the smithy and sit by the forge.

Ernest hobbled behind the group as they drifted into the warm building.

It was the damp of the night before, he told himself, that was making him feel so old and so lame. If he were a horse, someone would have taken a hammer to his forehead before now. It crossed Ernest's mind that growing old was a cruelty. That old people were allowed to continue soldiering on with their ailments and aches, without someone giving them the mercy of oblivion, was just an added woe.

You didn't allow animals to suffer. When an animal grew old and couldn't move around you put it out of its misery, but a person just had to keep carrying on.

They entered the forge, and he was instructed to sit on a stool by the fire. The warmth did help to ease some of his aching joints. He even managed to wriggle his swollen fingers.

The fat man with his kindly face sat down opposite Ernest.

"My name is Colonel Bainbridge, and I think you probably know why we are here. You are fully aware of the situation that has been occurring at the tower just behind this smithy?"

Ernest nodded his head.

What else was there to say?

"We have discovered your secret, Ernest. There is a tunnel leading from that old stall in the stables right to the base of the tower and ending in a forgotten dungeon that Mr Hollobone always speculated existed. But it doesn't contain the secret Bungay treasure everyone expected. Instead it contains the ill-gotten gains of a smuggling operation, one that I am certain has been operating for a great number of years."

Ernest remained silent.

"I don't think you are a violent man, Ernest," Bainbridge persisted. "I think you are probably someone who has just been caught up in all this nonsense. I also doubt you are clambering up onto the top of the tower to throw rocks at people. So why don't you just tell us what has been going on?"

Ernest shrugged his shoulders solemnly.

"It all started so innocently; I never even gave it a thought. One day, when I had just started working here, I was told to clean out the old storage area that hadn't been touched in years, and when I did, I came across the cover for a well. It looked like a trap door into a cellar. The bolt was all rusted in place, but I was able to oil it sufficiently that I could open it. I was younger then and more adventurous. I worked out that the old well was not very deep, and I went down it, that's when I found the tunnel."

"And back then, what was at the end of the tunnel?" Hollobone asked keenly, pencil poised over a sheaf of paper.

"Nothing, just an empty space. Some bits of the tunnel roof had fallen in, but whoever built it had done a pretty good job of shoring it up. It just intrigued me really. When I realised it ran under the castle it was rather exciting. In my spare time, I made the effort to make the tunnel safer. I had plenty of time at night when I was all alone here."

"That explains the discovery of the tunnel. But what about the smuggling?" Bainbridge asked.

"One night, when I had been working in the tunnel, I came up out of the well and stumbled on a couple of men who were trying to rob the forge. It was my purpose to be here at night as a watchman, but because I had been in the well, I hadn't noticed them until it was too late. I shouted at them, thinking they would bolt, but instead they rushed at me wielding some of the iron tools they had lifted from the smithy. I panicked and quickly hastened back into the well. At first they were laughing at my fright. They said they were going to shut the trap door over me and bolt it. They would seal me in, and no one would find me because no one knew the well was there. Frightened, I told them they mustn't do that, because no one but me knew of the well shaft and its tunnel, and if they shut me in I would surely die.

"One of them was a bit brighter than the other, who was still determined to shut me in. The clever one became curious. He wanted to know about the tunnel and the dungeon at the far end. At that point, I was caught between a rock and a hard place. I wanted them to let me up out of the well and I wanted them not to beat me about. Finally, I convinced them to come down to see the tunnel for themselves, which they did. They asked me all sorts of questions about it, and I showed them how I had shored up the walls and made it safe.

"How was I to know that it gave them an idea of a place to store their stolen goods? I thought when they left it was all over. I closed the trap door, bolted it shut and told myself I'd be much more careful in future. Then a couple of nights later, they came back. This time they demanded to know if I had told anybody else about the tunnel. When I said no, they were satisfied. They told me I was to say nothing and that they were going to use that tunnel as a secret hiding place. I would let them in at night and make sure that the well was kept concealed during the day. In return, they wouldn't cause me any harm."

Ernest shook his head sadly.

"What was I to do? I slept above the stable. I was vulnerable to them. Even if I had gone and told someone, they had plenty of friends around who could hurt me. And who would believe me, anyway? They had left behind everything they tried to take during the robbery. All I had was my farfetched story.

"No one would be able to do anything to them. They hadn't done anything wrong as far as the law saw it, and I if I talked, sooner or later someone would come for me and do me great harm. These were bad men. Terrible men. So I agreed. Over the years, they stored all manner of goods down in that dungeon and no one ever found them."

"And this smuggling ring has been operating all this time, all these decades?" Victoria said in astonishment.

"Not continuously," Ernest explained. "The first fellows who began it, well, they're long dead. One was shot trying to steal from a house. Another got into a fight and was stabbed, and another drank himself to death. I suppose they were only using the dungeon for seven or eight years. Maybe a little longer. Afterwards everything went quiet, and I pretended that the world and the tunnel did not exist. Then one day, this man came along with that same plan of the tunnels that your fellow has in his hands."

Ernest pointed at Mr Hollobone.

"He wanted to know about the tunnel. He came when I was the only person here. It was a Sunday. I remember it well. He badgered me into telling him where the entrance was, and I showed him. Those first fellows had only ever stored in the dungeon bits and pieces they stole from homes. They weren't really smugglers. But this new fellow, he was clever, and it was quite clear he had his fingers in a lot of pies. Suddenly my little dungeon was full of all manner of goods."

"How does this connect with Ethel Ward? How did she get hold of these plans?" Victoria asked.

Ernest had no answer for her. He just shook his head.

"All I know is that for years this has been going on. The man in charge of it all doesn't come here often these days. He used to come every couple of months, now it is more like a couple of times a year, but he has agents who come on his behalf. These agents bring his goods here and then move them on. Everything was done discreetly. There aren't any houses with windows overlooking this direction, so it was easy enough to hide everything at night, especially in the early hours. All was going fine until Mrs Ward passed away and the tower was sold to Lord Brooksby. Then he became uneasy. He was nervous that the tunnel might be found, and someone would learn about his secret."

"A valid fear with all the building work occurring, all it would take was someone to notice the dungeon windows hidden by the grass and to become curious," Bainbridge nodded his full understanding. "So he tried to scare people away using the myth of the phantom in the hopes that no one would get too close, and the workmen would refuse to work around the tower."

"Who is this man?" Lord Brooksby demanded. "Who murdered my father?"

"I am deeply sorry about your father, your lordship," Ernest said quickly. "Had I known he was going to do something like that, I would have put a stop to it sooner. But I didn't. I thought the only person whose life was at risk was me."

"Right under my own nose," Mr Fenton said furiously, his fists clenching dangerously.

"Not now," Bainbridge said to him swiftly. "There will be time for recriminations later, Ernest, you have to give us the name of the gentleman responsible for all this."

Ernest nodded his head slowly.

"His name is Mr Young," he said without hesitation. "I do not know where you will find him. I have never known his address. I barely know his name. But I can describe him to you."

"You better do just that," Bainbridge agreed.

Ernest started to give them a description of the man, making it as detailed as he could manage. None of them recognised the person he described as anyone they had seen about the area. When he was finished, Victoria shook her head sadly.

"How are we to catch this fiend when we don't know who he is other than a name?"

"We begin by attacking him where it really hurts," Bainbridge said firmly. "The first thing we are going to do is contact the relevant authorities and inform them about this smuggling cache. They will immediately decide to clear the place out and put plans in place to do so. There must be hundreds of pounds worth of goods down there and when Mr Young sees that his tobacco is on the verge of being seized he will likely attempt to retrieve it first. I have no doubt he has someone around here keeping an eye on things for him, who will report back on the situation. I suspect he will also react with anger towards the person he believes betrayed him."

Ernest understood immediately what was being said.

"He is going to come for me," he sighed.

"Ernest, you will be as much bait in this trap as the smuggled tobacco. We will need you to watch for the arrival of Mr Young and his men and alert us to his presence. We shall not allow any harm to befall you, you have my word on that."

Ernest nodded his head sadly.

"It is for the best. I never wanted to be a party to murder. I shall do everything I can."

"Then we begin by sending a message to Her Majesty's Customs and see to it that all these goods are seized. Once that is done, Mr Young is bound to come out of the woodwork."

"And I will finally have my father's killer," Lord Brooksby said with satisfaction.

Dreary was glancing at his men.

"You'll be wanting someone to keep an eye on Ernest to catch this fellow. We're all willing to be here," the foreman said.

"I thought you might say that," Bainbridge smiled at them. "Well, let us get on with things. The sooner we get this done, the better."

Nineteen

Bungay did not have a vast police force. It was a quiet town with little crime, but there was a local constable and a sergeant who were stationed there to keep an eye on things. They were summoned by Bainbridge and the details of the situation explained to them. Once they had heard all about it, they were quick enough to react and before long they had managed to get word to the nearest office of Her Majesty's Customs.

Word spread even faster after that, having reported to a senior officer, the sergeant swiftly had a division of policemen from Norwich arriving to hold the fort until the customs officers could arrive. Not long after they had descended on the town, the local police inspector turned up.

He had heard on the grapevine about what was happening and saw its potential for furthering the career and prestige of anyone involved. How often was such a large smuggling ring uncovered these days? This discovery could only look good for him, and the fact he had not been required to do any work for it was even better.

By the end of the day there was a whole collection of policemen and locals watching as Dreary's workmen brought up some sample barrels from the forgotten dungeon for the benefit of the inspector.

It seemed impossible that Mr Young's informers could have missed seeing what was going on. Surely by now, Bainbridge postulated as he thought about going back to the inn for his supper, he had to be aware of what was occurring and that all his goods were about to be confiscated. The problem was there was no evidence in the dungeon of the man himself. If he was clever enough, and Bainbridge couldn't deny that was a possibility considering how long he had been running this operation without anybody interfering, then Mr Young might simply cut his losses. He would realise that in attempting to retrieve his property from under the noses of HM Customs, he would place himself in greater danger. A sensible man would stay away, knowing there was no evidence to link him to this crime and he could disappear into the shadows as easily as the phantom he had pretended to be.

What they were relying on was that Mr Young's pride would be stung and he would act rashly and impulsively. His anger and humiliation would push him to confront Ernest and try to salvage something of what was left in the castle dungeon.

Bainbridge would have liked to remain at the smithy overnight, ready for the arrival of Mr Young, but Victoria insisted that they go back to the inn. Firstly, she thought it was better for the sake of anyone who might be watching if they left – they did not want Mr Young suspecting this was all a ploy to catch him.

Secondly, she was concerned that Bainbridge had started to snuffle and sneeze again; when she had discreetly placed a hand on his forehead, she had notice he was feverish. He needed to be indoors, he needed to rest. Had Bainbridge been feeling a bit healthier himself, he would have argued with her, but indeed he did feel as though he would prefer to go back to the inn, at least for a short time.

Mr Savage made sure they had a hearty meal of chicken with dumplings before them. They quietly ate, even Victoria tucking in to her food for once. She had been so cold and damp over the last few days that she had worked up an appetite.

Once the meal was consumed, they sat in silence, waiting impatiently for the moment they would learn Mr Young had taken the bait. Bainbridge stroked his chin thoughtfully, staring into the fire that crackled and burned. They hadn't bothered to light the gas fittings in the room, so the fire was their only source of light, creating a cosy, comfortable atmosphere. He was thinking of Ernest. Hoping he would be sensible enough to stay close to Mr Dreary and his men so that nothing could happen to him.

"Could this Mr Young be the man who was living upstairs in Ethel Ward's house?" Victoria asked after a moment.

Bainbridge had no answer for that. Just what sort of a man was Mr Young? A casual criminal or one who ran an entire gang? And how had he become connected to Mrs Ward? Bainbridge had met with a lot of villains over the course of his time as a detective, and he knew they came in all shapes and sizes. He also knew many would have no qualms in threatening a lone woman into using her cottage in secret.

The time dragged by; Victoria noted on the nearby clock that it was now nearly ten. Bainbridge was slowly dozing off in his chair. She wasn't going to disturb him as he needed to rest. She just hoped that they were right, and this Mr Young would walk into their trap. She was not sure how else they would catch him.

It was nearly eleven when there was a knock on the door to their room. Victoria rose hastily to answer the summons, trying not to disturb Bainbridge. Mr Savage was stood outside.

"Would you like a pot of tea before my wife goes to bed?" He asked her politely.

She had advised him earlier they might have late night visitors with information for them, and he had promised to keep the inn open as long as was necessary. So far, the evening had been perfectly quiet.

"No, thank you, Mr Savage," she smiled at him, masking her disappointment that he was not bringing news about their trap. "I take it there have been no messages for us?"

"Nothing, but I haven't locked the inn door, so if someone comes they can get in to speak to you," Mr Savage informed her before he bid her goodnight and headed off to his own bed.

The inn was falling into peace and quiet. It was not the sort of place where the customers stayed late, drinking into the wee hours. It was a place where people liked to have their meal and then find their beds early. Victoria stood quietly in the doorway and listened to the sounds of nighttime nothingness about the building. She was beginning to wonder if their plan was going to work.

She returned to her chair and sat down, leaving the door open so she could hear if anyone entered the inn. Bainbridge was snoring in his usual baritone. She didn't mean to close her eyes and drift off, but the warmth of the fire and the exhaustion of the last few days caught up with her. Besides, she had an unusually large meal in her stomach and was feeling quite content.

The creak of the inn door opening behind them suddenly aroused her from her dozing state. She half-opened her eyes, aware that someone had snuck into the room rather than knock and wake them. As the person approached closer, she stayed perfectly still. At the point when they were nearly by her chair, she suddenly rose to her feet and spun on them.

She found herself confronting an uneasy Mr Woolmer. He looked dishevelled; his clothes were damp and dirty, and the edge of one sleeve was torn. Wherever he had been hiding it clearly had not been a comfortable place. His hair, what was left of it, stuck greasily to his scalp and he looked as though he was frozen to the bone, in fact,

Victoria was sure she could hear the chatter of his teeth.

"Mr Woolmer, you must perch by the fire at once," she informed him, taking his arm and leading him to the fireplace.

She perched him on the hearthstone with his back to the gently glowing ashes. The fire had died down, but there was enough warmth to begin to bring some life back to the unfortunate caretaker.

The movement had alerted Bainbridge. He opened his eyes to see what was going on.

"Why, if it is not Mr Woolmer!" He said, looking at the man now perched on the hearth with his legs crossed before him.

Mr Woolmer hunched up, looking a mournful, dishevelled creature.

"I didn't know who else to turn to," he said, mumbling through his shivering teeth.

"We assumed you intended to simply disappear," Victoria said to him.

Mr Woolmer shook his head.

"I panicked when I realised what was going on," he responded. "But I never intended to go too far. I tried to hide around the town, keeping to outbuildings and barns. It's very cold at the moment."

Victoria suspected, though she didn't say it aloud, that it was the weather that had brought Mr Woolmer back to them, rather than a guilty conscience. She wondered whether, if the crimes had occurred during the summer rather than winter, he would have been so quick to turn back to them. Mr Woolmer had never lived an outside life and his experiences while on the run had clearly impressed upon him that he was not designed for life as a fugitive. He had been cold, wet, and hungry the entire time, and he had not liked it.

"Why don't you tell us why you decided to come back to us now?" Bainbridge said quietly.

"I came because I wanted to tell you what really happened. I need to tell you, and I felt you would be the best people to speak to. I can't face Lord Brooksby. My guilt is too much, my shame too heavy."

"He deserves to hear what you have to say more than we do," Victoria responded to him.

Woolmer shook his head.

"I simply hope that you will explain it to him. I have considered some dark things over the last couple of days. Even contemplated doing away with myself. I have done a terrible thing and though it was not through my own choice, it still hangs heavy over me, a burden I must bear to the end of my days."

"Why don't you explain this burden to us?" Bainbridge asked quietly.

Woolmer nodded his head solemnly. He looked exhausted.

"Not long after I was given the role as caretaker at the cottage, I was introduced to a man. He said his name was Mr Young. He came to the house one day, early in the morning, before anyone else was around. By that point I had thoroughly explored the place, and I had discovered that there was one room that had a locked door I could not open. I'd gone through all the keys in the property and none of them fitted it. Imagine my surprise when Mr Young turned up with the very key to that room.

"As he spoke to me, I began to realise just how dangerous a man he was. He never directly made a threat against me, but it was implied. It seemed wise to quickly come to an arrangement with him. I was not to go into the room upstairs, the locked one. That room would be maintained for the sole use of him or any of his associates he sent with the key. He wanted to know all the details about Lord Brooksby's plan for the tower. I didn't see any reason not to tell him. It was fairly public knowledge. Besides, he did not seem a man you said no to.

"He impressed upon me that I ought to say nothing about his presence to Lord Brooksby or anyone else. He smiled all the time we talked, but his eyes were cold, and he did not have to elaborate that there would be consequences if I did not obey him. It seemed innocuous enough, just ignoring that room upstairs, and so I agreed to the arrangement as much as anything, because I felt rather alarmed by the gentleman's presence, and I was alone at the cottage. I suppose I could have told my employer, but I did not want to lose my position. I have never had my own property before, a whole cottage to myself. I liked the place. I liked the thought of retiring there and I saw no real harm in keeping the secret."

"How long was it before you realised that Mr Young's intentions were far from innocent," Bainbridge said, knowing full well that Woolmer must have had an inkling right from the start that Mr Young intended harm.

How could he not? He must have wondered what was going on in that locked room upstairs.

"It was a few weeks after he had first approached me. Another gentleman came to the house, a younger man. He had the key. He looked a thug, but I said nothing when he told me he was going to be using the room upstairs. I simply let him in. That was the first incident when people said they saw a phantom on top of the battlements. I kept my mouth shut on the subject.

"This young man spent many days in that room. He would leave for a time, then come back. When my late employer, Lord Brooksby, was killed by a falling piece of masonry from the top of the walls I had a suspicion of where it had come from. I even found the courage to ask the young man. He told me that it had been an accident. He had been leaning over the battlements to see what was below and a loose stone had fallen. He couldn't prevent it and there was no point in saying anything because we would both be culpable, wouldn't we?"

"So you remained silent while this young man continued to masquerade as the phantom and tried to sabotage the work at the tower," Victoria said grimly.

"I extracted a promise from him that he would not do anything that could seriously harm anyone again. He swore he would be more careful, and, for a time, that seemed to be the case. It was a near miss when he dropped that stone on Matt, but it did only catch his shoulder, and he told me it was because the gentleman had moved at the last moment. But then Billy was killed, and I can't help but feel that that was deliberate."

"Mr Woolmer you are culpable in this matter by failing to warn others of the danger," Bainbridge told him calmly. "You could have prevented the murder of Billy. You will need to explain this to your employer and to the police. Your only hope now is in aiding us to catch Mr Young and his accomplices. That will perhaps limit the punishment you receive for turning a blind eye to their activities."

"I cannot help you further," Mr Woolmer groaned miserably. "I do not know where you will find Mr Young. All I can do is tell you a little bit about him. He is an older gentleman with a rounded face. He walks with a stick and is hunched over. You might almost suppose he had a kindly appearance, but deep down he is an evil soul."

This was not getting them any further and Bainbridge was growing frustrated. He was determined to press Woolmer for further information when there was a sudden sharp knock on the door. They had been so occupied they had not even heard footsteps approaching.

Victoria hastened to the inn door and opened it. She immediately recognised Mr Dreary who was looking rather sheepish as he stood before her. There was blood running from his nose.

"Mr Dreary! You look a state! Come in at once."

Victoria ushered the unfortunate man to the room where her uncle and Mr Woolmer were still sitting. He was dabbing at his nose with his sleeve.

"I must apologise for my appearance."

"Nonsense, Mr Dreary, you have clearly been in quite the affray tonight."

Bainbridge jumped up from his chair the second he spied Dreary. Mr Woolmer ducked down as best he could before the fire, trying to pretend he was not there.

"Mr Dreary! You must have a drink!"

Bainbridge was moving to the bar of the inn to get Dreary a stiff drink as Mr Savage appeared from upstairs.

"Did I hear someone at the door?" He asked before he suddenly saw Mr Dreary and froze in surprise at the sight of him.

"Mr Savage, if you would not mind, could you supervise Mr Woolmer who is in the taproom? I doubt he will try to leave, but it would not hurt to have someone watching over him."

Mr Savage was bemused by the request, but he obeyed without hesitation.

Bainbridge handed Dreary a shot of whisky and the foreman downed it fast, wincing as the movement sent new pain rushing through his bloodied nose.

"We have someone," he said, his voice slightly muffled as he tried to snort back blood. "A fellow came after Ernest just about half an hour ago and we have him tied him up in the stable. He's going nowhere."

"Then we shall come and speak to him at once," Bainbridge said firmly.

Without hesitation, he and Victoria followed Mr Dreary all the way back to the smithy.

Ernest was wandering around in the smithy yard, looking agitated, and managing to stumble back and forth despite his rheumatism. He made his way over to Bainbridge and Victoria the second they came in.

"It is not Mr Young, but one of his cronies," he told Bainbridge.

Bainbridge patted his shoulder, promising that he would now take charge of the matter, and headed to the stables. In one of the stalls, now empty of its former equine occupant, stood two of Dreary's workmen. They had their arms folded and were guarding someone lying on the floor between them. The man had been tied up with rope around his arms and chest. His feet had also been tied together and he had a gag in his mouth. However, he did not need to be able to speak for Bainbridge to realise exactly who he was.

"Well, well," he said, looking at the man on the floor. "If it isn't Mr Crookshaw's butler."

The story began to unravel after that. Mr Woolmer was summoned to the smithy along with the police. When he identified the butler as the man who had been sent by Mr Young to act as the phantom things began to fall into place.

As soon as the sun was up, Lord Brooksby was summoned and Woolmer, along with Ernest, were both taken in the carriage to the home of Ethel Ward's cousin. They were greeted by a footman on the doorstep because, of course, the butler was absent. The footman immediately informed them that his lordship was unwell. Bainbridge would hear none of it. He managed to push his way into the house, the presence of Lord Brooksby backing him up and causing the footman to scrabble out of their way. They went to the library, where they once again found Mr Crookshaw sitting at his table in his Bath chair.

"To what do I owe this unpleasant intrusion?" He demanded of them.

Bainbridge did not answer him, instead, he looked at Ernest.

"Would this be the man you know as Mr Young?"

Ernest glanced in the direction of the gentleman in the Bath chair and simply nodded his head.

"And what of you, Mr Woolmer? Do you know this man?"

Mr Woolmer took a good look at Mr Crookshaw and then said quite firmly.

"That is Mr Young."

"What is this nonsense?" Crookshaw responded.

"We are here, Mr *Young*, for I shall call you that as it is the name you prefer to go by when committing your crimes, because we have your butler in our custody. He is probably at this very moment telling the police all about your schemes. How you used the tower and its hidden dungeon that your cousin owned to house smuggled goods and that once your cousin died, you wanted to continue your scheme."

"You're speaking nonsense," Mr Young chortled at him. "If I was using the cottage as a secret place, why would I sell it?"

"Because what you told us was genuine. Your cousin did have a lot of debts that fell upon you when she died. You had to find a way to pay them off, but a great deal of your own wealth is caught up in your smuggling business. You had to make a choice. Did you use some of your illegal profits to pay her debts? Or did you sell the place? It was a risk, but you hoped that the buyer would be more interested in the ruins than the cottage. In any case, the tunnel did not connect with the cottage, and you hoped to keep your business activities a secret. In actual fact, having someone else on the site probably would have provided you with extra cover. But things went wrong.

"Lord Brooksby decided to begin restoring the tower, and you realised that ultimately someone would notice the small slits at the base of it that allow light and air into the dungeon. You found yourself in a difficult position. I would hazard a guess that your smuggling operation has not been as profitable these last years as it used to be, with the changes in the law removing taxes on the items traditionally smuggled into the country, your illegal business was no longer providing you with the revenue you had grown used to. All these things taken into consideration, the sale of the cottage was essential. But you had not banked on Lord Brooksby's grand schemes.

"The extensive restoration work at the tower required you to act. You decided to use the secret way up onto the battlements to try and spook Lord Brooksby and the workmen into leaving things alone. It had been a useful lookout point in the past to keep track of when goods were entering the town. Your cousin had kindly ensured that the upper floor was never entered by anyone but your associates, to aid another layer of protection to your secrets and the rumours of a phantom had worked well in the past to keep locals away.

"However, Lord Brooksby was not one to be superstitious and did not take the phantom seriously. You told your butler to begin his murderous stone throwing activities. He began to throw masonry down to put the lives of the workmen at risk, but that still didn't stop Lord Brooksby. So he threw a stone at his lordship. Perhaps he really did not intend to hit the man and kill him. Whatever the outcome, Lord Brooksby was dead. You had to have hoped that was the end of things, but of course his son decided to continue on with the project and you had to continue on with your scheme to scare him away."

"What a load of nonsense," Mr Young grinned at him. "You might have noticed that I am a housebound gentleman. I have no interest in the tower or smuggling."

"We have two witnesses who will make it very plain that you are not housebound, that you are fully capable of walking, albeit with a stick. We also have your butler in custody, and I wonder how long it will be before he decides it would be in his best interest to reveal you? I generally find that when people are already of a low moral fibre they are more interested in saving their own skins than caring about their employer's. Despite your attempts to threaten people, I doubt you have that much hold of over *him*. It is over, Mr Young."

Mr Young glanced between them. There was a moment when it seemed as though he was considering jumping up out of his Bath chair and making a run for it. Then he realised the ridiculousness of such an attempt.

"I just wanted them to stop trying to restore the tower," he shook his head, realising the game was up.

There were too many witnesses, too many loose ends and his entire operation had just been shut down.

"My cousin, Ethel, was not the only one prone to mounting up debts. I just needed one last good sale of my illicit goods to try and cover my own expenses. I am an old man. I don't want to be in this smuggling game anymore. But I had to do something. I suppose I had dug myself into a hole.

"Ethel knew about the smuggling, of course. She found it romantic, daft woman. Sometimes, my agents would need somewhere to spend the night after their travels to Bungay bringing or taking away goods. She let them use the upper rooms of the cottage, never let anyone up there in case they noticed someone else had been there. My cousin was good at keeping secrets."

Mr Young sunk down in his Bath chair. He suddenly looked extremely ancient and frail.

"It was never meant to end like this. I am very sorry about everyone who has died. I never set out to be a murderer or to encourage murder. It is a terrible thing to have occurred. I never wanted that to happen."

"It will be necessary for you to convince a court of law of that, not us." Bainbridge told him.

Off to one side, Lord Brooksby was looking sadly at the man in the Bath chair.

"You killed my father," he said quietly. "I shall never forgive you for that."

The police were summoned, and Mr Young was arrested. The full story soon emerged when the police began questioning his butler. Mr Young's resolve had failed him. He felt old and tired, and he was plagued by remorse over the deaths that had happened at his instigation. Murder had never been his intention.

With Ernest and Mr Woolmer as witnesses against him, there seemed no doubt that he would end up facing a jury along with his butler. The days of the murderous phantom of Bungay castle were truly over.

Lord Brooksby drove Victoria and Bainbridge back to the inn. He sat opposite them looking solemn.

"I am sorry it was not a better outcome," Victoria said to him.

Brooksby simply shook his head.

"What other outcome could there be? I wanted you to find my father's murderer, and you did just that. I never expected to feel happy about it. But I do very much appreciate what you both did for me."

"What are your plans for the future?" Bainbridge asked him.

"First things first, I am going to finish the project my father started. The tower will be restored; however, I shall not create the additions that he desired. It simply will be shored up and opened to the public so that they can learn about its history, and I shall make sure that the dungeon can be reached from the tower floor. There must be another way into it other than that tunnel we discovered."

"You certainly have a good story to tell about the ruins and that will no doubt bring people to see it."

"It shall be my father's legacy, and I think it will be a worthy legacy. I hope it will bring him peace wherever he is now to know that his death was not in vain, and that the tower will serve the purpose he desired."

He deposited them on the inn's doorstep, and they waved him goodbye. Then it was Victoria's job to get Bainbridge safely home. It was another wet day, and the rain blew in through the open sides of the car as they travelled home. They were both slightly damp when they finally arrived.

Bainbridge walked through the front door and Victoria could have sworn that he planned it perfectly to sneeze just at the moment Mrs Huggins appeared before him.

Mrs Huggins was aghast to see the colonel suffering with a cold. She grabbed his arm, scolded him for not returning at once and told him he was to go up to his bed and remain there for the next week until he was fully recovered. She completely ignored Victoria, though she was also damp to the bone and was beginning to feel a little feverish herself.

Victoria knew her place.

Bainbridge made no protest as he was ushered away by his housekeeper to begin his convalescence. Victoria was left to sort herself out. That was just the way things were, and Victoria didn't mind too much. She was not that keen on being fussed over, especially by Mrs Huggins. She could already hear Bainbridge giving instructions of all the delightful food he would like to eat while he was recuperating and Mrs Huggins turning on him and telling him he was going to consume beef tea until she was satisfied he was on the mend.

Victoria smirked as she heard Bainbridge protesting and regretting how quickly he had revealed his illness to the housekeeper.

Victoria stripped off her damp clothes in her bedroom and slipped on her dressing gown, deciding that she too would resign herself to bed, having not slept properly for quite some time. Before she tucked up beneath the covers, however, she wandered over to her bookcase. She fingered along the line of novels on the top shelf until she came across one that she had never read, but which she knew was there. It had been a gift from someone a long time ago. She pulled it out and looked at the cover with its gold imprinted letters spelling out the title.

The Bungay Tower Mystery by Ethel Ward.

Victoria smiled at the book. She started to move towards the bed, then she hesitated. Ethel Ward was involved in smuggling, no matter how indirectly. Ethel Ward had a lot of secrets and maybe her suicide had been due to her guilty conscience after all.

After a moment of indecision, Victoria put the book back and selected another instead.

The Gentleman Detective Mysteries

Have you read them all?

The Gentleman Detective

The first mystery

The Unholy Preacher

The second mystery

The Unwelcome Guests

The third mystery

The Last Word in Pickles

The fourth mystery

The Mayfair Mystery

The fifth mystery

Murder on Ice

The sixth mystery

The Man of Friar's Wood

The seventh mystery

The Cherry Tree Murder

The eighth mystery

The Mystery of Cromwell's Skull

The ninth mystery

The Return of Turpin

The tenth mystery

The Fatal Gathering

The eleventh mystery

Also by Evelyn James

The Clara Fitzgerald Mysteries

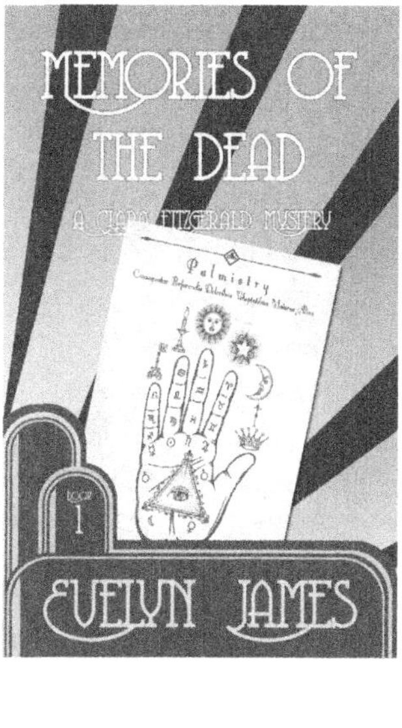

Memories of the Dead

One murder. Two suspects. Bad things happen when you mess around with a mother's grief.

Clara Fitzgerald is struggling to make her name as a private detective in 1920s Brighton, when most people think women cannot solve crimes. Undaunted by the prejudice she faces, she sets out every day to her humble office in the hope someone will ask for her help.

Then she meets Mrs Wilton; a scatter-brained, emotional widow who believes her dead husband can lead her to lost treasure from beyond the grave. Ignoring her better judgement, Clara is drawn into the case. There is nothing she detests more than people abusing another's grief and that is exactly what a fake psychic is doing to Mrs Wilton.

Wanting to help and understanding Mrs Wilton's grief all too well, Clara makes a promise to aid her. But when matters take a dark twist, Clara finds herself accused of murder. Can she prove her innocence, along with proving herself as a detective?

Memories of the Dead is the first novel in this cosy, entertaining, historical murder mystery series by Evelyn James.

If you love engaging, quick-witted, no-nonsense female heroines solving dastardly, mind-boggling murders – and doing it all while armed with no more than a sharp hatpin or fire poker – then you'll love Evelyn James' page-turning, 1920s, detective series.

About the Author

Evelyn James (aka Sophie Jackson) began her writing career in 2003 working in traditional publishing before embracing the world of ebooks and self-publishing. She has written over 80 books, available on a variety of platforms, both fiction and non-fiction.

You can find out more about Sophie's various titles at her website **www.sophie-jackson.com** or connect through social media on Facebook **www.facebook.com/SophieJacksonAuthor** and if you fancy sending an email do so at **sophiejackson.author@gmail.com**

First published by Red Raven Publications 2024

Evelyn James is a pen name for Sophie Jackson.

To contact about licensing or permission rights email sophiejackson.author@gmail.com

Printed in Great Britain
by Amazon

53157795R10121